Allan Baillie

MEGAN'S STAR

PUFFIN BOOKS

Puffin Books
Penguin Books Australia Ltd
487 Maroondah Highway, PO Box 257
Ringwood, Victoria, 3134, Australia
Penguin Books Ltd
Harmondsworth, Middlesex, England
Viking Penguin Inc.
40 West 23rd Street, New York, NY 10010, USA
Penguin Books Canada Limited
2801 John Street, Markham, Ontario, Canada, L3R 1B4
Penguin Books (N.Z.) Ltd
182-190 Wairau Road, Auckland 10, New Zealand

First published in 1988 by Thomas Nelson Australia
Published by arrangement with Blackie and Son Ltd, Great Britain
Published in Puffin, 1990

Made and printed in Australia by The Book Printer

Baillie, Allan, 1943-
Megan's star.

ISBN 0 14 034046 7.

I. Title.

A823'.3

Contents

1
Megan

Megan was a tiger in attack. She flashed her teeth. Her nostrils flared as the tiny bumps of the basketball scudded across her fingertips. She could scent the kill.

'Meeg!' Little Pam was scuttling out wide, clear of the panting pack and toward the crooked hoop. But Hornsey was charging between them, a snorting elephant, her runners squealing on the macadam.

Megan shot the ball hard under Hornsey's massive arm, skipped sideways and ducked forward. Hornsey faltered, but she was too big and too fast to change direction. She thundered past as Pam snatched the ball on the run and Megan leapt at the hoop. Megan was almost growling.

Perfect. The last defender was drifting in from the side, but she was too far away, too slow. Hornsey was trying to come back, but she was still reeling, sliding away. Pam was lifting the ball, her fingers shifting behind it, but her eyes were on the hoop, not Megan.

'Pam!' Megan clapped her hands from the peak of her leap.

Pam flicked her eyes from the hoop to Megan,

back to the hoop and to Megan with a trace of reluctance. But the ball spun into Megan's hands. She steadied in the air, cocked her arms as the hoop slid toward her—

Help!

Megan blinked and turned sideways, the ball still nested in her hands. 'What?'

She slapped her right foot down on the macadam, took two stumbling steps and stared past Pam's astonished face to the school building.

There was something . . .

Wasn't there?

Three storeys and an attic of scorched brick darkened with age. A black-tiled gable roof, steep enough to defy any landing bird, a forest of chimneys that hadn't seen a fire in half a century. Many narrow windows but no face behind them. It was deserted now, apart from Mrs Larkins, her bitter detention class and the cleaners. There was nothing there.

The leader of the other team, Captain Alice, was shouting very loud, but that wasn't it. It had been ice cold and far away. But clear, very clear. And frightened.

Perhaps something in the Morton Bay Fig, the giant, shadowed tree that broke the grey sea of the schoolground? Even older than the school, it kept a tribe of possums. But it had not been a possum sound and there was no face peering round the tree, nothing disturbing the leaves.

Hornsey was running away, bouncing a ball and whooping.

Something outside the grounds? In a house, or a passing car? If the sound had come from a car, it was gone now.

Hornsey's ball rolled round the other hoop and dropped through. Hornsey yelled in triumph and Megan suddenly realized that her hands were empty. She dropped her arms.

Captain Alice caught the ball, hung it on her hip and smiled graciously at Megan. 'Bad luck, Megan,' she said. 'You gave us a good game.'

Little Pam glared at Captain Alice and said: 'Next time.'

'Oh, certainly,' said Captain Alice. 'But I have so many things to do. 'Bye.' She jogged easily to her bag.

Little Pam nodded and muttered at Megan out of the side of her mouth: 'Whatever did you do that for?'

Megan was still looking about her. 'I just can't hear anything now. Do what?'

'Give the ball to Hornsey the Grisly. Give! Like it was a box of chocolates.'

Hornsey snorted behind Pam. 'Ah, Old Meg was making up a spell to zap us with.' She walked away with a bunch of laughing mates.

'I would never give chocolates to Hornsey,' Megan said loudly. 'Not one.'

'Well you did, didn't you?' said Pam.

Megan looked at Pam as if she had just discovered the short brown girl. 'Did you hear it?'

'Hear what?'

'You didn't hear it, did you?'

'Oh, Meeg!'

Megan shook her head. 'You'd know if you heard it.'

'I am going home.'

'Well I did hear something.'

'What sort of something?'

'A boy's voice, something. I don't know.'

Pam looked back at the quiet basketball court, the school, the sagging wire fence. 'No boys here. Anyway, so what?'

'Calling for help.'

Pam looked hard at Megan. 'Oh.'

Megan hauled her eyes from the rusted weathervane on the school's roof to Pam's troubled face. 'What do you mean, "Oh"?'

'Hornsey was right.'

Megan felt her face tighten. 'I knew I'd get that from you. Thanks very much.' She snatched up her bag and wheeled for the gate.

'It was a joke. A joke,' Pam called after Megan. 'You're not in fairyland again?'

Megan slowed.

'Are you?'

Megan strode through the entrance and slammed the gate behind her. 'Not this time,' she said.

2
The Hunters

Megan crossed the road quickly, putting space between her and Pam before she stopped at the foot of the steep S-curve of Victor Street. She swept her eyes across the old terraced houses, the uneven paving of the footpath, the reeling telegraph post a block away and the green wrecked van, now resting on its hubs. No one in the street but Laslo painting his wall high on the hill. She tilted her head and listened.

She lifted her left foot, touched a small pebble and heard a faint click. She could hear her breath, a little strained, a cat swatting a dead leaf in a cobweb three houses away, and a man singing softly in Greek in the next block.

But nothing like a young man whispering desperately in your ear.

Let's stop it, shall we?

She rubbed her nose, straightened and started to take the hill with a cool, reasonable walk. In case anyone was still watching.

They never stop, do they? As if you were silly in the head.

She strode a little faster.

Why don't they just boil their heads? All of them.

Megan slapped her rubber soles past the heavy spiced aroma of the Pappadoulos house—do they cook all the time?—jumped a fallen garbage tin and thrust handfuls of air behind her.

Hornsey is so unfair. Taking the ball then, when anyone could see you had stopped playing, and then gloating about it, dragging up the old history.

Sweeping up the hill with her knees creaking beneath her, the panting back again, aiming for the leaning pole—some teenager had driven down Victor Street as if it was straight—and Laslo's wall.

But you heard it, didn't you? Just then, back there. Didn't—

Megan caught a toe in a pavement ridge and sprawled.

'Hey, hey!' Laslo came away from his wall, paintbrush dripping and pulled Megan to her feet. 'You okay? What is the matter with you? Think you gonna fly?'

Megan looked at her scraped palms and hung her shoulders about her ears. 'Thanks, Laslo. I got a bit angry.'

'That's no good. Don't get mad, make them get mad at you instead. That's plenty better.'

Megan tried a smile and looked up at the sun-wrinkled, paint-splattered scarecrow of a man. 'Did you hear any funny sounds?'

Laslo passed his hand through his thinning, white-streaked hair. 'No, but I hear surf now.'

'Surf?' Megan glanced at Laslo's wall, the high brick barrier before his tiny terrace house.

Laslo's wall was his passport to the world and anyone walking the street was invited along for the ride. He would paint a picture on the wall, leave it for a few months then paint the wall white and create another picture. On that wall had been an Austrian castle, a windjammer going round the Horn, the Sphinx, Victoria Falls, Mount Everest, Rheims Cathedral, the Nile and the Grand Canyon. There had been very few slogans sprayed on that wall. Now there was Hawaii.

'Oh, I like that,' Megan said. 'Have you really been to all the places you put on the wall?'

Laslo tilted his head. 'Nah. I have never been to any of them. Hey, but I can dream . . .' He stopped and nibbled at the handle of his brush. 'Maybe next time I do Budapest. It is a long time.'

'Your home?'

Laslo was not listening. 'No, not long enough. It is better I paint places I have never seen.'

Megan left Laslo with her walk slowed to a dawdle and her anger almost put to sleep. But sometimes, she thought, I wish I could really cast a spell.

She stopped before a chalked hopscotch grid and hopped once.

I don't know why I waste my time with any of them.

Hop, hop, straddle.

Little Pam was all right until she got on TV. Now it's: 'Do you think I'm getting fat, Meeg?' 'Got to watch the sun, Meeg.' 'Be careful of my hair.' Maybe I'm jealous. Just a little.

Megan bounced over the squares, stopping with a thump that echoed down the street.

Hornsey—now she should be given a TV job. As a bear rug. And Captain Alice. Nobody calls her Alice Windsor any more, except the teachers.

13

She is school captain, team captain, whatever. Everything she says comes from some captain book. 'But I have so many things to do.' Probably wears her prefect badge to bed . . .

'Excuse me, miss.'

Megan started. A dark blue car had slid silently into the gutter on the wrong side of the street and a dark-eyed man in a crisp suit was looking up at her. One of the new cars with rotary engines and no sound. This one looked like it was designed for stratospheric flight, not for the side streets of Balin Dock.

'Looking for something?' The dark-eyed man glittered in the green light of the round video screen set in the dashboard.

She stepped nervously away from the car. 'No. Nothing,' she said.

'We're looking for something.' The dark-eyed man smiled at Megan but there was no warmth in his face.

'Oh.' Megan glanced sideways at the nearest corner, but it looked terribly far away.

'You live locally, miss?'

'No . . . I mean yes.' Megan caught a movement beside the dark-eyed man and saw a smaller man staring at her from the shadows in the car. He seemed to be wearing a suit as well.

'Well, what do you mean, girl? Do you live here or in the bush?'

'Here, just round the corner. Mum's waiting for me.'

The dark-eyed man glanced at the video. 'Bates Street? That's all right. We'll only keep you for a few more moments. Have you seen anyone odd around here today?'

14

'Well . . .' Megan had not really seen anyone, just heard—or thought she had heard—a cry. She was looking at the suits, pressed, spotless, shades of grey with quiet, almost identical, striped ties, and there was something wrong about the men. 'Are you police?'

The two men looked at each other. 'Of a kind,' said the dark-eyed man.

'You were going to tell us something, weren't you?' the other man said.

'Of a kind' means they are *not* police, Megan thought. 'I don't know what you want, sir. I was trying to think.'

'Strange people. People you haven't seen before. Have you seen strangers around here lately?'

Megan nibbled a fingernail. 'Well, there's been a man pushing an old trolley full of junk, trying to sell it. But he always comes round every few months. And there were a few men wrecking the old house in Dalgleish Street, but they've stopped now. And there's a strange old woman just moved into one of the terrace houses . . .'

'Ah, give it up Vic,' the smaller man said. 'She doesn't know anything.'

The dark-eyed man sighed. 'Thank you, miss. Good night.' He turned the car out of the gutter and it slid silently on up the hill.

'And then there's this strange voice . . .' Megan said softly.

She hesitated. Home was straight ahead for two blocks and turn left, but the car had gone that way. She turned and ran past Laslo, back to the now-deserted school, and walked quickly along its length. She almost stopped near the basketball

15

court to listen and she did stop at one of the slender H-pillars of the sky-train to get her breath back.

She hadn't told the men a lie, really. Only she hadn't told them the whole truth. But what if she had really heard the cry, someone being kidnapped or something, and the men were trying to save him. You don't like the men, why? Because they wear suits and drive a flash car?

The pillar vibrated briefly against Megan's back. She looked up to see the sky train hissing softly toward the city, a ribbon of light against the gathering dusk.

Doesn't matter. Nobody heard it. It didn't exist, like the purple cloud. Mrs Gleason is going to kill you.

Megan slapped the pillar and ran up the narrow footpath of Dalgleish Street, past the ancient stone warehouse and the empty woolstore, the decaying terrace houses and the house that had been partly knocked down and left like a hermit on a hill. Ahead a very old man leant on his brick gate post and stared out at the street, unmoving, as if he was not seeing anything. Or seeing things that nobody else could see. Dalgleish Street had a strange air about it, as if it was full of ghosts.

Megan thought she spotted the blue car in the distance and pressed herself into the gate recess of the house and panted a bit. The old man winched his eyes toward her, chilling her with the slowness of his movement. He finally turned his head to her but he kept staring, staring through her. When the car turned off Dalgleish Street she ran all the way to the warmth of her street.

The noise and the smells of Bates Street poured

over her in a wave. The Tarini family was cooking fish, the Osborne couple were eating Spaghetti Bolognese, the Chows were arguing with Mrs Fahed over a front fence and Adrian Thomas was taking his car apart in front of his father's house. Here you could forget about strange cries and sinister men. Everything was normal and safe.

Megan stopped outside the freshly-painted brown and white house half way along the block. She straightened her uniform, marched up to the door and raised her knuckles. An annoyed woman jerked the door open.

'About time, Megan Dawson. I'd just about given you up. Come on and take your beastie away.'

3
Goblin

'I'm sorry, Mrs Gleason, I got held up.'

Mrs Gleason propped her arm on her heavy hip. 'Basketball or boys?'

Megan flushed. 'Two men kept asking me questions.'

The arm dropped. 'Oh. Did they frighten you? Where are they now?'

'They said they were policemen.'

'Are you in trouble?'

Megan shook her head. She shouldn't have mentioned the men at all. 'They wanted to know some things. I think they were after burglars.' That should do.

A grimy small boy pushed a plastic fire-engine between Mrs Gleason's feet, looked up at Megan and grinned. 'Brrm-brrm, bee-ba, bee-ba! Hi Meeg! Brrum-brrump!'

'Hi Walter. Ready to go home?'

'Did these men say who these burglars had robbed? How many of them were there? Are we in danger? They should warn us about these things.'

Megan scooped Walter from the carpet and balanced him on her hip. 'They didn't say. Just

18

wanted to know if I'd seen anything. I've got to go. Sorry. Bye.'

'It would be the Thomas family. They'd have been burgled but nobody would ever know. They'd have a murder in that house and never say a word.' Mrs Gleason nodded toward Adrian Thomas' dismantled car and closed the door.

Megan moved towards the gate as Mrs Fahed shouted at Mr Chow something about 'stealing my land!' and kicked at the new dividing fence. Mr Chow was looking about him in embarrassment but Mrs Chow was shaking her head as if a plague of mosquitoes were whining about her nose. Teen-aged Rosalind Fahed looked out of her second-storey window at Peter Chow in his second-storey room and showed the land their parents were fighting about in the space between her fingers. She shrugged and Peter threw his arms over his head in despair.

'I'm hungry, Meeg,' Walter said sadly.

''Course you are, Goblin. You're hungry all the time.'

Megan walked from Mrs Gleason's freshly-painted brown and white house to its neighbour, a terrace house with ornamental ironwork rusting above and a front wall of grimy stucco scarred and chipped back to the old bricks.

'Hi Adrian,' Megan said as she creaked open her gate.

A ginger-haired boy, his face blackened with grease, waved a spanner at Megan from under the car. 'It keeps on dying. The monster.'

'Sell it?'

'Hah! Who's gunna buy?'

19

Megan shrugged and stepped to the front door. The door was the colour of spider webs, there were cracks from the edges and the knocker by the shiny slot was so badly broken it was a trap for the unwary visitor. The front window was starred from a pebble thrown by some kid a long time ago. But it was clean. You could say that about the house at least. The front window was clean, because Megan had washed it last week.

'What we gunna eat, Meeg?'

Megan placed herself before the shiny slot in the door and told it: 'I am Megan Dawson, thank you.'

The shiny slot said: 'Thank you. Welcome Megan Dawson.'

Megan turned to her brother. 'I dunno, Goblin. What d'you want?'

The slot hummed, clicked and the door swung open. Dad's last gift to the house.

'Ah . . . pizza. And chocyluf ice cream, and—'

'You'd be lucky.' Megan bundled Walter into the dark corridor. She turned the light on, sighed and stepped after him.

It was now 4.30. She had ninety minutes to clear up the house, feed Goblin, warm the house, get Goblin to bed and prepare the meal before Mum—always tired, always bad-tempered—came home. She would worry about writing that silly composition about the old wharves later in the night.

She walked past Walter and down the corridor, with its single picture of a loopy girl sniffing flowers, through the crowded sitting room and into the yellow kitchen. As usual the kitchen looked as if a bomb had exploded in it. In the morning Megan was always late for school because

20

she was tired, and Mum was late for the library because she had to make sure she looked right. They made coffee while eating muesli and washing Goblin's face, and frying eggs, and buttering sandwiches, and combing Goblin's hair. They had gulped and run, leaving almost everything on the table, in the sink, on the benchtop, on the chairs, on the floor.

'Ug, warra mess,' said Walter brightly.

'Shut up, Goblin,' Megan said absently as she started to fill the sink with water, mugs and loose spoons. She turned on two of the coils of the cooking range as she passed it.

Walter sat down heavily. 'Hungry.'

Megan opened a few sheets of newspaper on the benchtop. 'It's coming. What tremendous things did you do today?'

Walter was not satisfied. He glared blackly at his big sister, sniffled, trembled his upper lip and took a great breath.

Megan pointed at him with a wooden spoon. 'Do that and I'll brain you with this. Okay?'

Walter subsided mutinously.

Megan pushed two saucepans under the tap, half-filled them and turned the tap off. She poured some rice into one of the saucepans, placed it on a coil and dropped a packet in the other saucepan as she put it on the range. She began to scrape the dirty dishes into the newspaper and felt that she was getting somewhere.

But Walter had opened the pantry and had crawled inside. A rolling crash shook the floor.

'Goblin!' Megan leapt for the pantry.

Walter had pulled a bottle of lemonade down

from a lower shelf, spilling half a bag of flour over himself and the floor.

'You ghastly little man!' Megan shook Walter by the scruff of the neck and stamped her foot on the floor in anger. She blew hair back from her face and brushed the flour from him with deliberate calm. She dumped him out of the pantry while she picked up most of the flour with a mug.

Walter was a little annoyed. 'Thirsty,' he said.

'You could have asked.' Megan poured Walter a glass of milk and went back into the pantry with a brush and shovel, then with a damp cloth.

Walter was blowing bubbles in his milk.

Megan slapped him across the leg. 'And don't you move this time.'

'Brumm-brummp,' said Walter.

Megan finished scraping the dishes and began to wash them.

It is all a pain, she thought. The whole thing. Mum carries on like everything is late and wrong and it's all your fault. You go to school and Miss Larkins shovels homework at you like she is filling a laundry basket. And lines—I must not talk in class, I must not talk . . . and there goes the lunch hour. And when you get out there's always Roger. Just the world's greatest nit-wit, that's all. All apologies and offering chocolates. And that means you have to put up with Little Pam and the other girls for the rest of the afternoon. Isn't he sweet, Meeg? It's so *romantic*, Meeg. Keep him around and he'll give you a diamond ring. And when things begin to look good for a bit, when you're flying with the ball and you've left Captain Alice and them all in a heap, then you have to hear funny little voices so you lose it all. It's all a pain.

But the dishes were done and the rice was bubbling. It wasn't all that bad.

'Goblin,' Megan called. 'Time for dinner.'

Silence.

Megan turned and looked at the back of the kitchen. Goblin was no longer there, just a powdery patch and faint trail leading to the open door.

'Goblin, I told you to stay here,' Megan said tiredly. 'Where are you?' She reached for the bubbling rice pot.

'Goombang!' shouted Walter, and a heavy crash rocked the house.

Megan ran from the kitchen and into the living-room.

Walter was sitting in the hearth of the old fireplace with a brass poker on his knee, a demon king. The boy and the area around him were covered with thick soot. His eyes flashed whitely through the black and he was grinning.

Help me. Please.

Megan stopped in mid-shout and closed her eyes, suddenly trying to hear what she could not see.

Then Mum strode into the house.

4
Flight

'What have you done!' shouted Mum.

Megan turned from the tall angry woman at the doorway, from Goblin, quiet now as he realized that he might just be in trouble, and tilted her head to the window.

'Why must I come home to this? What sort of game are you playing?'

'I can hear, I can hear . . .' Megan clapped her hands over her ears to cut out her mother's shouting.

'That's all you can do!' Mum took a stride toward Megan, then sniffed, dropped her bags and bolted for the kitchen.

'Where are you?' Megan said softly.

Goblin inspected the soot over him and hid behind the protection of a sudden bawl.

Mum rushed back out of the kitchen and slapped Megan's hands from her ears. 'Don't you ever do that to me! Come here and see what you've done!'

Mum grabbed Megan's left arm and hauled her into the kitchen where the two pots were still overflowing on to the dying hotplate coils.

'You're supposed to be growing up? You're getting worse. Look! Just look at what you've done

24

tonight. The kid—shut up Walter!—he's filthy, the room's filthy and I don't know how we'll get both of them clean again . . .'

The woman—she was a stranger now—trembled violently and flung Megan's arm from her. 'I suppose I should be grateful that you haven't burned the house down.'

'But someone's in trouble,' said Megan, only half hearing what was being said.

'Oh, you've worked that out? You just clean up that mess and I'll get Walter into the bathroom.'

'But I heard it . . .'

Mum shook her head and hit Megan across the face. 'Don't play games! Get on with it! Sometimes I wish your father was here.' She pushed Megan toward the range and stamped out of the kitchen.

'So do I,' Megan said.

'What did you say?'

'Nothing.'

Megan cleaned the hotplate with her face stinging. She felt a low pleasure when a slap echoed from the bathroom, crowned by an outraged yell from Walter.

'Well?' she hissed as she dished the rice in rings on the plates, and tried to listen for something strange and faint. There was nothing but the shouting and splashing from the bathroom.

I heard nothing, she thought. Nothing at all. Crazy little girl.

Megan snipped the packet open and poured the meat and the onions into the centre of the rings, and took the plates to the table.

Mum carried Goblin to the table, glowing, sulky and ready for bed. She dumped him on the high chair, sat and stared at the meal Megan had placed before her. Megan looked away and waited for the abuse.

But it didn't come. Not yet.

Mum slowly lifted a forkful of rice and gravy, put it in her mouth and lowered the fork. Her arm was trembling.

'Sorry. It's not much good, is it?'

Mum shrugged. She looked tired, worn. Fifteen years older than when Dad had left, only two months ago. 'There were some children in the library today . . .'

Goblin pushed at his plate.

Mum's fingers were whitening on the fork, as if she had to have something to hold onto. 'Giggling—smoking in a corner—you tell them they have to leave and they won't go and what can you do? Call the police?'

Megan began to relax. 'Why not?'

'I caught two of them drawing moustaches in one of our art books. Animals.'

'That's—'

'I just can't get away from them, can I?'

Walter dropped a loaded spoon on the floor.

'Come home and the kitchen is a pig-sty. . .' Mum's voice rose and quivered '—the meal is burning black. Walter is in the fireplace—what were you doing, making a fire of him?—and you're playing one of your silly games . . . There's no relief, ever.'

Megan shook her head violently. 'That's not fair! You want to see Gob—Walter when you're not at home. He does things all—'

'And I'll tell you something, girl. You wish your

father was here, well, so do I! To get some sense out of you.'

'Good!'

'Right!'

'I'd get some justice in this house!'

'You'd get—if you want him so bad, whyn't you go with him? Eh?'

'I will! I bloody well will!' Megan lurched to her feet in an explosion of sliding, toppling plates, skidding table, crashing seats and angry roar.

Blinded by tears, Megan bolted from the shouting. She reeled down the corridor, bouncing between the walls until she burst from the house.

She hesitated only at the gate, blinking the mist from her eyes to see Bates Street still and dark now, Adrian's car leaning with a rag trailing from under the boot like a tongue, the second-storey windows of the Chows and Faheds vacant and black. A street of shadows and bolted doors.

'Mee-gaan!' Mum shrieked the length of the corridor and the width of the street. Megan stumbled past the gate and ran.

Past Mrs Gleason's tidy little house, out of the street, twisting right for a long downhill run, taking greater strides, leaning back but gaining speed. Whispering of the air flowing past, the flat slap of runners on concrete, no other sound in the street, no one else. Too fast to think.

The old man, he's still there, looking at the road, looking at you. Doesn't he ever go in? Pass him, quickly. Like that. There's someone else running. Behind! It's the old man. Old men can't run that fast. It's Mum! Coming to drag you back by the hair and rub your nose in the mess. Run faster.

27

She's running faster too, step for step. Don't worry about the panting. Past the wrecked house, the old rotting houses, the old woolstore, the tall warehouse and she's getting closer. Can't keep going. Where is she? There's no one there. Stop.

Just an echo.

Megan propped her body on her knees and coughed weakly. After a few minutes she walked unsteadily under the sky-train and toward the gleam of the still black water.

She wiped her eyes clear and was a little surprised to find she had been crying. 'I'll never go back,' she said.

She shied away from a park bench when she saw a ragged man asleep, and realized where she was. She had bolted to the tiny piece of park in the waterfront, her afternoon refuge, without thinking of it. When she had suffered a bad day at school or weekend at home she would come here and watch the rusty little freighters being loaded on the backwater wharves until she had almost forgotten what it was that had troubled her. Dad's disappearing act had kept her here for an entire day. And she was running after him, now! As if she could ever find him.

And before was during the day, when everything was familiar, with kids shouting a block away and the big man in the crane sometimes waved at her. But this was at night, when every sensible girl was at home watching TV, when raggedy men slept on park seats and rowdy gangs ran along the streets, rattling fences and looking for trouble.

She should be home.

Megan walked to the old scarred stone wall that

28

rimmed the quiet water. She hunched on the wall and looked down at her face, reflected in the moonlight. Just a pale face with a long nose and a wild tousle of brown hair, but the dark eyes looked a little frightened—like a cat's, when you yell at it.

What to do now?

The anger was gone now, leaving her cold and uncertain. She tried to stoke the ashes of its heat.

It was Mum's fault, wasn't it? It always is. Comes home from the library and she always wants a fight. You can't get out of it, no matter what. If you got Goblin fed, bathed and in bed, did the dishes, cleaned the house, painted the walls, cooked her a roast duck followed by chocolate mousse and coffee, she'd still want a fight. Cinderella Meeg, that's what you are, all Mum has to do is turn Goblin into two ugly sisters. That's all right, so long as you get to change the teapot into a white pony.

Megan stopped. There was something in the air, something she could almost hear. She heard the man snoring on the seat behind her, the water lapping against the wall and the buzz of the electricity in the wire overhead. Nothing else.

You'll have to go back.

She's probably still shouting. You don't want to go back. Stay here.

She wasn't always this way, was she? No, just lately. Just since Dad left. Doesn't matter. She is this way, now.

And then Megan heard the voice, very faint, soft and distant.

Please . . .

5
Kel

Megan turned from the water, but she knew there would be nothing to see.

'Who are you?' she whispered, softly so the man on the seat would not wake.

Nothing. She strained her ears until they hurt, but she knew the voice was beyond hearing. 'Where are you?'

I'm hurt. Like a tickle in the head.

'Where are you?' She was shaking now.

I don't know.

He doesn't exist, Megan thought. Just a piece of your imagination. Can't you see that? Crazy little girl.

But she said: 'This is no good. You must know something about where you are. Or I can't help. Please try.'

Nothing but the buzzing of the wires.

'Come back,' Megan raised her voice and the ragged man snorted in his sleep. She moved away. 'Say something.'

Hurting.

'Where? Where does it hurt you?'

My back. Legs. Arm.

'Did you fall?'

No.

'Were you hit with something?'

Yes.

'A car?'

The roof.

Megan took a quick breath. Perhaps this is real. Perhaps, perhaps . . . 'You are in a building?'

Nothing.

Megan tried again. 'Are you in a building?'

Are you alone? Nobody is with you?

'No. But I can get help.'

No!

'All right, all right. You are in a building. Are you near me?'

I do not know where you are.

Megan closed her eyes. 'What sort of building?'

Please?

She looked out of the park at the massive brick warehouse. 'Big stone building?' How do I find him in one of those? How do I get into one?

Not big. It is a small house. It was a small house. It is finished.

Megan frowned, then looked up. 'Finished? You mean wrecked?'

I am hurting . . . please help . . .

Megan hurried from the park, her feet ringing softly on the empty footpath. 'I think I know where you are. Just keep talking.'

Nothing. A lean black cat skittered over her feet, yowling at a raggedy woman crossing the street with a grocery bag.

Megan walked toward the sky train. 'Say something.'

31

The raggedy woman plucked some cut meat from the bag and offered it politely to the cat.

'Don't just sit there and wait,' said Megan.

'Eh?' The woman stopped in the gutter and squinted.

'Sorry Bea, just thinking,' Megan hurried past.

'Silly girl!' Bea the Cat Woman muttered. 'Ought to be safe at home.' She would be feeding her stray cats for most of the night.

The sky train buzzed over Megan's head, now a jewelled spear flung toward the distant city.

'Come on, I am trying to reach you,' breathed Megan. 'Just tell me if I'm getting closer.'

Hard to think now. Do not know where you are. Stone is pressing on my back . . .

'I am in Dalgleish Street. It runs downhill to the docks and the sky train. There are old warehouses down the hill. Do you remember that?'

I think so. But I was running—it is moving!

Megan stopped and listened with her eyes wide and fixed. 'All right? Are you all right?' She ran up the hill of Dalgleish Street, panting and scything the air with her arms. A small dog started to bark and disappeared round a corner.

Megan reached the ruined house in little more than a minute and leant against the gate post, staring at the rubble.

'Are you there?'

Bricks sticking from the walls of neighbouring houses, a half-wall hunched over a pile of masonry, old beams pointing at the moon like a wolf howling, a withered tree bowed sadly in a corner. Nothing moving, no sound at all.

'You must be there. Please.'

I'm . . .

Megan swung open the gate, hesitated a moment then walked toward the ruin. She climbed three worn stone steps and jumped carefully between two heaps of bricks. Something rattled down the heap to her right, bouncing lightly on her shoe.

'Can you hear me? Can you hear me now?'

Megan reached for a splintered piece of wood to steady herself and it crashed down beside her. She fell sideways, propping herself on a broken piece of plaster and sitting painfully on a bent pipe.

'You're not here at all, are you? You're in some other wreck, in some other suburb. Maybe in some other city, hey?'

Or you don't exist.

Megan staggered to her feet and moved clumsily near the broken wall. More bricks, stone, tumbled in piles and an overgrown back yard with an old tyre hanging from the withered tree.

'You're not here. There's nothing but broken bricks here. You're playing games and I'm going home.'

Megan turned and snapped a piece of window glass with her shoe.

I can hear you!

Megan stopped, crouched and looked around her. 'I can't see anything. Anything at all . . . oh.'

A shoe, twisted and empty, half-buried in a mound of rubble. Megan reached for the shoe and saw a foot sticking out from a collapsed tunnel of bricks, then the leg, the other leg, the body of a man—a small man—almost buried face down by stones, broken bricks, fragments of cement and wooden framework.

33

Megan was shaking now, in a strange mixture of excitement, fear and relief. You're real! You actually exist!

She lifted a piece of flooring carefully from the back of the man's head and his hand came awkwardly away from his ear.

'You all right?' Megan said cautiously.

Thank you. The man twisted his head sideways and worked his mouth. 'I am alive. I think,' he said.

Perhaps not a man, Megan thought and moved closer. Perhaps just an old kid.

But he had been bleeding from a cut over his cheekbone, his hair was so matted with dust it was impossible to pick the colour, his legs were covered with bricks and a great chunk of sandstone lay across his back. Part of the remaining wall had come down on him.

'I don't think I can move the stone,' she said quietly. 'I'll get help.'

'No!' His voice was hoarse and tired, as if he'd been shouting in a wind for hours. 'You can do it. Come on, try.'

'I can get someone in a minute. Just a few seconds.'

The boy shook his head. 'It's not that. Just lift.'

'I don't want to hurt you.'

'You can't hurt me more than that is doing. C'mon.'

'Well . . .' Megan straddled the boy's back and tried to lift. The stone cut into her hands and the boy groaned and made a white fist. After a few seconds the weight shifted between Megan's strain-

34

ing hands and the stone settled on to the boy's back. The boy gasped.

'I can't do it. I tried,' Megan panted. 'Let me get someone.'

'Get two long, flat pieces of wood. There must be something.'

'What? Oh, levers.' Megan searched the rubble and found two window ledges.

'Now stick them—'

'I know where to stick them.' Megan shoved the ledges under the corners of the stone on the boy's back, jammed the ends of the ledges under a pile of bricks, placed the other ends on her shoulders and heaved. The ledges bent like a bow and Megan gasped in pain.

'M-m-moving!' And the boy was clawing himself out from under the stone. Megan fell over backwards.

The boy smiled, said 'Thank you' and held his breath.

'Ooh, that really hurts.' Megan held her shoulder. 'You all right?'

The boy nodded, but he was staring at a brick before him.

Megan climbed unsteadily to her feet. 'Trouble?'

'I'll be all right.' The boy was breathing his words between his teeth.

Megan was casting around for things to say. 'I'm Megan Dawson. Who are you?'

'Kel. It's just that I'm not numb any more. Oh, hell.' He winced.

'Kel?'

'Yes.'

'Just Kel?'

'Just Kel.'

'Where d'you live?'

'Why?'

'Well, we have to get you home. Don't we?'

Kel grunted. 'Got no home. Not now.'

'You hiding?' Megan drew slowly back from the boy.

Kel looked at her with hooded eyes. 'Why do you say that?'

'Because you're here, in this wreck of a place in the middle of the night. Police after you?'

'No.'

'They didn't look like police.'

'Who?'

'Two men in a car, I didn't think they were police. But they were looking for some stranger.'

'That's me. They almost caught me out there. That's why I came in here, and everything fell on me.'

'What do they want?'

'I haven't done anything wrong. Really. It's what they want me to do. Look, it's complicated, I hurt, I'm too tired to think properly. Can I tell you about it tomorrow?'

Megan felt a little guilty, as if she had been caught playing Captain Alice. 'I'm sorry. You look awful. What do you want to do now?'

'Is there anywhere I can hide for a night here?'

Megan looked at the boy and found herself weighing him against what she'd seen of the two hunters in the car. 'Gee, I don't know. I could try to get you into our place, but Mum would kick up a terrible stink—'

'Oh, no. Thanks.'

'There's an empty woolstore and a warehouse down the road but they're locked.'

'They'll do.'

'But they're all padlocked and everything.'

Kel pushed painfully against the wall until he could get his feet under him. 'They'll do.'

Megan worked under Kel's shoulder and they reeled out of the ruin and down the street. She caught the thick acid smell of his sweat and wondered what on earth she was doing. Promenading down a lonely street with a strange—very strange—boy in the middle of the night, about to commit a crime. Now she was definitely a crazy little girl.

She stopped outside the woolstore, a double storey with a saw-tooth roof, a door and a broad iron roller—both massively padlocked. She pointed at the door and said: 'See? They're all like this.'

Kel stared at the lock and coughed. 'Open it.'

'I can't,' said Megan patiently. 'It's locked.'

'It's not,' said Kel.

Megan sighed and moved out from under Kel's arm and marched up to the padlock. 'See?' she said, holding the padlock in her hand.

The padlock sprang open.

Kel limped past her and pushed the weathered door open. 'Thanks. See you tomorrow.'

'How did you do that?' Megan said a little angrily. 'And how did you get into my head?'

'That's what they want me for. Goodnight.'

6

The Woolstore

Megan hesitated outside the door to her home. She imagined Mum waiting for her, crouched in the corridor with a belt dangling from her hand. Ready to scream at her, loud enough to echo down Bates Street, long enough to make the neighbours scream back. And then Goblin would shriek and Mum would hit out and . . .

Megan muttered her name at the door and it opened quickly. At least she had not been locked out.

The house was quiet but there was light flooding into the corridor from the kitchen. Megan breathed heavily and walked slowly to the kitchen. Mum was sprawled over the kitchen table, eyes closed and an open book under her right hand. There was no sign of the plates hitting the floor or her toppled chair.

'Hi Mum.'

Mum blinked at the light, focused on Megan's face and pushed herself up. 'What's the time?'

'I don't know.'

'Doesn't matter. Get to bed.'

'I'm sorry—'

Mum waved Megan quiet. 'We're all a little bit too tired. Go on, off to bed.'

Megan turned, surprised and weak with relief, and moved back along the dark corridor to her bedroom.

'Megan,' Mum called.

Megan turned with her shoulders hunched, waiting to be cut down.

'I'm glad you're back.'

* * *

Next morning the family was quiet. Mum cooked scrambled eggs and talked brightly about a woman who was convinced that someone was using her library card on the sly. Megan laughed politely and made honey sandwiches and Goblin kept on gazing at her as if he was expecting her to throw things around.

'Aren't you making a little too many sandwiches?' Mum said.

'I get really hungry at lunch time,' Megan said quickly.

'Looks like you are feeding the entire school.'

'Oh, no . . .' Megan pushd the sandwiches into her box rapidly, shoved in two apples and whipped the lid in place, before she stocked Mum's box.

They ate the scrambled eggs in a hurry, as always, but the atmosphere was almost relaxed. For the first time Mum didn't talk about Dad and his absence did not cast a shadow over the family meal. Maybe things were getting better.

As Megan shoved her undone homework and her heavy lunch into her bag Mum swept the dishes into her arms and made a little run to the sink. Then she turned and looked at her daughter with worry in her eyes.

'You all right?'

'Yes. Sure, Mum.'

Mum lowered her eyes to the bag. 'You're not doing anything silly, are you?'

'Silly? What d'you mean?'

Mum shook her head. 'Doesn't matter. I've seen too much silliness from your father and I'm seeing it everywhere. Go, you'll be late.'

So Dad hadn't been forgotten yet, Megan thought with a little surprise. He still hurt.

She hurried down the corridor and into the street, turning quickly away when she saw Mrs Osborne kiss Mr Osborne at their door. She turned the reaction into a glance over her shoulder, making sure Mum hadn't followed her on to the street. She hadn't, so Megan sprinted towards Dalgleish Street instead of taking her normal route to school, past some mysterious chalk marks outside the Chows' fence and Rosalind Fahed talking in a furtive huddle with Peter Chow at the Dalgleish Street corner.

'Hi Ros,' Megan said brightly as she passed them. Mustn't look guilty.

'Oh, hello Megan.' The tall, dark-eyed girl rippled her fingers casually at Megan, but she was blushing as if she had been caught shop-lifting.

Megan smiled, but the smile died as she walked down toward the distant wharves and saw that the old man of Dalgleish Street was again at his post. He was now looking away from her, past the woolstore toward the sky-train, the harbour and the glinting city. She placed her hand on the lunch box.

He's going to see you. He's going to see everything you do anywhere near the woolstore. Did he see you last night?

Megan hesitated, then crossed the road to the side of the woolstore so at least the old man wouldn't see her going out of her way. But she couldn't deliver the sandwiches under his eye, could she?

A plump girl in a flashing kaftan turned into the bottom of Dalgleish Street and walked toward Megan, plucking a battered guitar.

Judy, everyone knows Judy. Maybe the old man will watch her instead of you.

Megan slowed so Judy would pass the woolstore before she reached it. Judy lived in a one-room flat near the school, wrote her own songs and sang them in at the Bounty pub. Sometimes she sang the more respectable ones at the school.

'Hi, Big M. Teachers still getcha?'

'All the time, Judy. Any new songs?'

'Can't think of anything fresh Big M, that's the pity. This morning they are going to get the old stuff—really ancient. Seeya.'

And often she sang at the sky-train station as a busker.

Megan strolled on, fumbling open her lunch box and placing some sandwiches and one apple in the bottom of her schoolbag before closing the box. She reached the unlocked door and looked back up the hill. The old man had turned away from her to stare after Judy. Megan stepped to the door, opened it, placed the box inside, closed it and walked on.

'Hello,' she said softly. 'Are you there? Breakfast.'

41

Then she ran to school.

Nothing changes. Mrs Larkins gave a general tongue-lashing to the pupils who had been 'too lazy to turn off the television to work their brains instead of their bottoms for a change' and Roger saying, 'I would've helped you with the home-work, Megan. Just ask,' and Hornsey just sitting there grinning. Mr Lake stormed in promising to catch the 'louts who painted "skool stinks" in pink—bright pink!—on our wall'. And all you had to do then was write a short story using: metropol-itan police, hospital, elephant, court, charge and electricity. The ridiculous things they ask you to do.

Roger leaned across the aisle with his ears wiggling and his eyes bright.

'Yes,' Megan breathed quietly.

'Police courted an electric elephant called Metro Polytan . . .'

'Yes, Roger?' Mrs Larkins snapped.

Thanks for the sandwiches, Megan.

'Oh shut up.'

'Megan!'

'I didn't mean you, Mrs Larkins.' Very hastily.

What's wrong? Are you in trouble?

'You were still talking to Roger? Weren't you listening to me at all?'

'No.'

'What?'

'I mean—I have a terrible headache, Mrs Lar-kins. Right here.'

'I want to speak to you at lunchtime Megan Dawson.'

42

'Gee, I'm sorry Megan.' Roger hissed out the corner of his mouth.

What's wrong, Megan? What's wrong?

At lunchtime Megan did last night's homework and cleaned the blackboard. She didn't want to communicate with Kel and she didn't think she could, anyway. Kel did his silent talking trick only when he felt like it and he only felt like it when it would cause embarrassment. He would speak when she was talking to Hornsey, Little Pam or—he should be so lucky—Roger, or in the middle of an afternoon class.

But he didn't.

Megan scraped her sandwiches from the bottom of her bag and ate them just before the bell rang. She trooped into a geography class and only half-heard how glaciers carve mountains because she was listening for that strange voice in her head.

Little Pam dribbled a basketball before her after school. 'Want a game?'

'I've got things to do.'

'Hornsey says you've got too slow.'

Megan wrinkled her nose. 'Tomorrow.'

'Tomorrow's Saturday.'

'Monday then. Give her a chance to practise. I've got to go.'

Megan ran from the school to the wharves and slowed under the sky-train to a meander before the woolstore. She stopped before the tall warehouse, noted that her lunchbox was gone and looked up and down the street. The old man was not at his gate. She ran the three steps to the old door, banged the lever handle down and slithered into the building.

43

'Hello,' she called into the dark.

She took a small step toward a grey shadow.

And tumbled over and over, a doll flung into a pit.

7
Alcatraz

Megan stopped with a rattle and a thump. She was winded, sore, covered in dust and seeing little sparks of bright colour circling her head. She thought she had broken something.

'Kel?' she wheezed, but so faintly that she was straining to hear her own voice.

She closed her eyes until the coloured sparks faded and slowly picked herself up. Above her head the brilliant gold bar of daylight flooded under the closed door, and the grey slabs of wooden steps marched down to her feet. Around her were a silent gathering of shadows, broken only by the scattering of dusty needles of light that had escaped from the cracks in the ceiling and a stark black arch in a grey stone wall.

'Kel—where are you?' She tried again.

Sorry. I was asleep. Come on up.

She relaxed a little. 'Wish you'd stop doing that,' she muttered and then yelled it out. 'Wish you'd stop doing that!'

People will hear.

'Big deal.' She dusted her dress and was wondering what she could tell Mum to explain it, when something scuttled in the dark.

She ran up a few steps but forced herself to slow down before she reached the door. It's only a mouse, she thought. Isn't it?

But she was getting used to the gloom now. The basement or the cellar or whatever was still a coal pit, but the floor above was grey, not black, and it even showed solid outlines. She reached the door and stepped sideways on to the narrow stretch of floor and around a wide wooden slide that dropped into the basement from inside the roller door. She was now standing in a broad, high gallery, tall metal pillars standing in ranks to carry a green wood ceiling that was somehow rippling—like a surging sea.

'How d'you like it?'

Kel was calling down from a loft to one side of the main gallery, his voice echoing a little from the old stone walls. The metal columns had given way to heavy timber columns on this part of the gallery, and he was waving from behind one of these, looking like a long spider.

'It's all right.' Megan found the second flight of steps and stumbled over the two wooden rails nailed over them. Not again, she thought as she groped for the banister. She was sucking a splinter in her finger when she finally reached him.

'Boy, you move about like an elephant,' Kel said.

'You're not so good, either.'

Kel was sitting on a single discarded bale of wool, his shirt off and an ugly black-purple bruise covering most of his lower back.

Megan eased past rough shelves still carrying a few old books and yellowed papers and looked again at his bruise. 'Sorry,' she said. 'That's bad, really bad.'

'I don't feel like running about. That's a fact,' Kel said.

'You must see a doctor.'

'And have the glum twins pick me up. Oh no. Nothing's broken and it's getting a little better already.' Kel moved very slowly to his feet, favouring his right side. 'See? Look, thanks very much for helping me last night.'

'That's all right.' She moved closer to Kel and was surprised to see that he was clean, cleaner than her. The rumpled dusty savage of last night had been washed and combed into a cool-eyed boy, dusky brown and lean under a clump of light brown hair.

'And for the sandwiches. Can you get some more?' He tapped the side of his broad nose in thought. 'Maybe some milk.'

'I'll try.' Megan picked at the splinter.

'And fruit. Lots of fruit, apples, bananas, grapes, yes, grapes. A book or two. What about a towel and clothes? Anything from your dad.'

'He's not here any more.' Megan tried to get a nail under the splinter.

'Who?'

'Dad. How long are you going to stay here?' Megan waved her hand around at the woolstore. She could see the boy could be causing her world of trouble.

'Ah, I don't know. It's a pretty neat place, this.' He started to wave, winced and nodded instead at the ceiling over the gallery. 'There's inbuilt light here, sometimes even a bit of sun—'

Megan could see now that the ceiling of the woolstore did not ripple at all. But it was broken by rows of small vertical windows, forcing it to follow a sawtooth pattern. The windows kept the gallery and Kel's loft airy and fairly well lit.

'And there's a great bed.' Kel kicked lightly at the bale. 'Maybe the only one in the place, I dunno. I haven't really explored yet. And they even left me something to read.' Kel pointed at a few dusty invoice books on the shelves. 'And there's a roof if you can get to it, and a sink.'

Kel grabbed his shirt from the hook where it had been drying, and led Megan to a small room by a very primitive lift. The room contained a sink, a dripping tap and a toilet.

Megan prodded the cracked but damp cake of soap in the bottom of the metal sink and turned the tap to blast the sink with rust-coloured water. She worked at the splinter in the water.

'They'll never catch me here. I can stay here for months.'

'This is silly. Just what do they want you for?'

Kel looked at Megan. *I am a bit of a pest, aren't I?*

'Stop that! How do you get into my head, anyway?'

'I'm not really. I'm just broadcasting and you are picking it up. I don't know what you're thinking.'

'That's something.' Megan tried gnawing at the splinter in her finger. It wasn't moving.

'Unless you are broadcasting.'

Megan looked up sharply. 'How do I know when I'm broadcasting?'

Kel took Megan's finger out of her mouth. 'Maybe I can fix it.' He turned the finger in his

48

hand and stared at it. 'Oh you do. It's when you throw a thought out of your head like a ball at a wall. Like this.'

And the splinter slid from Megan's finger, hovered in the air for a second and twirled to the floor.

Megan examined her finger. 'You know, that is a little fantastic.'

'Nah. That's easy.'

'That's how you opened the lock, then?'

'Sort of. But you have to look inside first.'

'How long have you been doing things like that?'

'Since I was six. First thing I can remember is rolling Mum's thimble round on the table so she couldn't catch it. They thought the house was haunted.'

'So the people who are after you, they want you to do things.'

'Bunch of researchers. Mad scientists. They want me to do tricks for them. They found out about me when Mum got herself into a screaming panic over me floating the cat in the lounge, and raced me off to the doctor. The doctor shoots me off for an ECG—you know, a graph that shows how much the brain is working. For most people two thirds of their brains just sit there like a hen waiting for the gold egg to hatch.

'But mine, oh no, mine is racing round my skull, looking for a way out. "Hmm," the scientists say, "this is very interesting. Do you mind, Mrs Rader, if we take this boy to a special city school to find out what his brain is doing?" School? More like a jail. Worse than a jail. Alcatraz. "Oh yes, Dr Hemings, take our little Kelway, drug him, stab him with your needles, poison him, cut off his head. Anything for science."' Kel kicked at a wooden pillar.

'It can't be that bad,' said Megan.

'Ha! They put me in a dormitory with only an old man, a funny woman, another boy and a dog. That's all. The school is just a couple of hours in a room with a raspy teacher and the other boy who's bright but nowhere as bright as he thinks he is. You know the type, "I'd talk to you, boy, but you bore me." The old man is a stage magician and he thinks he is a wizard, guessing things on cards in another room. The woman—well, she'd go about telling everyone that the world was going to end—things like that. Seeing clouds over people—even on TV.'

'Clouds?' Megan leaned forward. 'I—'

'Well they're not really there. She says they're there.'

'Little dark ones, sometimes green, sometimes purple? I have seen them.'

'Well, don't ever tell anyone about it!'

'I did once. But never again. Kids said I was weird.'

'This woman is. She said she could see the future but she was wrong so many times that even the scientists ignored her. The only good thing about Alcatraz was the dog.'

Kel smiled and Megan realized that it was the first time she'd seen warmth in the boy's face.

A special dog?' she prompted.

'Raffles was so smart they should have given him his own computer. They first saw him herding some cats like they were sheep, knowing what each cat was going to do even before the cat knew it.

They put Raffles in a room with four chutes for food and they'd change the chute all the time to try and confuse him, but he'd be waiting at the right chute every time.

'You'd play throw-the-stick with Raffles, and he'd play all right, but when you'd try to fool him, throw your arm out but keep holding on to the stick, he'd just sit there. Cock his red kelpie head as if he was saying, 'Come on now, Kel, get on with the game,' and then he'd run off and you'd decide to throw for real this time.'

'Wish I had a dog like that. Or a cat.'

'Oh Raffles was good. He was smarter than the scientists and he showed it. I would've stayed in Alcatraz, even with the experiments, if he was still there.'

'What happened?'

'Doesn't matter.' Kel walked to the stairs, stiffly and pressing his arm against his bruised side. 'When do you have to go?'

'Oh.' Megan looked at the long streaks of sunlight on the walls. 'I suppose now. I am sorry.'

Kel nodded. 'I won't come down with you, if it's all right. Still hurts a bit.'

Megan passed Kel and hesitated with her foot on the first step. 'What were these experiments? How bad were they? Worse than an exam?'

Kel laughed a little and held his side. 'Ooh, that stings. Maybe not as bad—sometimes. Trouble is they don't really know what they're looking for or how to find it. One great twit was trying to prove that some people can burn themselves away sometimes. Yeah, really. You are sitting there and you think a bit and—oops—you're a pile of ash. So

51

he's got some funny case histories and he wants us to experiment. What if we find out we can do it? Another one wants us to talk to ghosts.

'But it's mostly boring. Lying on a bed with a helmet on your head for hours, trying to read a book someone's reading in another room. I couldn't. Or trying to increase your pulse rate without moving. Or trying to affect a graph needle, or trying to detect a temperature change of half a degree. Just boring and who cares anyway? And you're doing these things for hours and weeks. And if you succeed in any of their funny little tricks they treat you like a freak. Oh no, I am not going back.'

'Get your parents to pick you up.' Megan sounded a little strange. 'That's what they're there for.'

Kel shook his head. 'No good. You going to bring the fruit, the food, books and something to wear?'

'Yes, yes. As soon as I can. But what's wrong with calling your parents?'

'They've got scared of me.'

8
Trap?

Megan felt a strange chill as she ran to Mrs
Gleason's house. She knew this neighbourhood;
she knew it all. Now, at this moment, Laslo would
be painting a wave on his wall, Judy would be
strumming her guitar at the sky-rail station for the
commuters, Adrian would still be lying under his
car, Captain Alice and Hornsey would be practis-
ing goal shots at the basketball court, Bea would
be chopping up the waste meat she had picked up
at the butcher for her stray cats, Bates Street would
be awash with the aroma of conflicting cooking
herbs, Mrs Fahed would be threatening the Chows
with lawyers and their kids would be plotting
away together.

Megan walked into the Old Man of Dalgleish
Street's stare almost without realizing it. She passed
the man a metre away and he kept staring down at
the distant water.

Everyone was still here and Megan knew them
all, even the Old Man of Dalgleish Street. Knew
where to find them, knew what they'd most likely
be doing, and sometimes why. Nothing had
changed, but everything felt different now.

Megan turned into Bates Street and saw Adrian

standing beside his car, grinning, listening to the beat of the engine. Standing in the street as if he was watching for her. She turned into the neat brown and white house.

'Hello, Mrs Gleason. How has Walter been?'

A cold and hostile stare. From the woman who knew everything about Bates Street. 'Nice of you to pay us a visit, Megan. He's as usual.'

Usual? No, no one is as usual any more. Not since last night. Now there are two strange men wandering the streets, hunting for a boy you know. That changes everything.

Goblin nuzzled Megan's neck as she carried him home, then bit at her ear.

'Stop it, pest.'

And it's because there are things—maybe very bad things—that you don't know about, but they are there, just a few corners away. A 'school' called Alcatraz which exists only to experiment with how some people's heads work. But that is silly. Silly as Bea.

But Megan hesitated and looked over her shoulder before she talked the front door open.

The dark blue car with the two men in crisp suits was gliding slowly along the street.

Megan stepped quickly into the hall and slammed the door behind her. She hurried into the kitchen with Walter shouting in her ear and caught herself trembling a little.

Oh, come on, they can't find anyone. Forget them.

She placed Walter on the kitchen floor and pulled some mince from the fridge.

What if they have something in that car that detects funny brains?

Megan stopped with a handful of flour over the chopping board. She remembered the time she looked at the young teacher, Henderson, and saw something in the air over his head. She had told Pam, Hornsey, all the girls, that she felt he would be in trouble soon. And next week he died in a car crash.

Walter made a noise like a crashing plane.

Megan turned sharply but Walter was sitting with his back to a closed cupboard and diving a dented duck on to the cork tiles. No trouble at all, but Megan found herself wishing Walter was covered in flour again, so she could stop thinking about things.

After Henderson's death the kids changed. Some of them started calling her a witch and some of them—like Hornsey—still did. 'Old Meg was making up a spell to zap us with.' 'Can I hitch a ride on your broom, Meg?' 'Watch it or she'll turn you into a frog.' But far worse, she could not get rid of the feeling that somehow she had killed him.

What had Kel said about being treated like a freak? She knew the feeling. She had not talked about any of her strange feelings since Henderson, and she had been sliding into a 'normal' mode until Kel had called her. Now she was remembering the cloud over Henderson's head, the ghostly whisperings of Dalgleish Street and her vision of a city that had not yet been built. She did not want any of that again and she wished that Kel had left her alone.

Maybe her head was funny enough to put her into his Alcatraz.

The front door slammed. 'Hello, hello!' Mum was stamping along the corridor.

Megan stared at the floury, uncooked heaps before her and hunched her shoulders. She started talking very fast. 'I didn't have time to—'

'That's all right, love.' Mum nodded and placed a flat white package on the table. 'No work tonight.'

Megan was puzzled. 'Pizza? What do I do with this?' Waving her hand at the rissoles.

Mum scooped Walter from the floor and rubbed noses. 'Put them back in the fridge. This is my treat.'

'Yes. All right. That's great.'

'You sound as if I never give you anything but a row. Doesn't she, Walter?'

'Gumta.'

'Sorry. You're early.'

'They owe me some time. I decided to take it today.'

'Why, Mum?'

'Never mind why. Get that cleaned up and we'll eat.'

Megan swept the flour and the rissoles on to a plate as Mum hummed and set the table, with Walter making faces from her shoulder.

You never know, Megan thought. One day Mum wants your head, the next she's giving a birthday party. Don't complain. No, but it would be good if Mum stayed in the middle of her moods most of the time, wouldn't it?

'Good day?' Mum lifted a cheese-stringed wedge of pizza and concentrated on a clean bite.

'Sorry?'

'Have you had one?'

'Oh, it wasn't bad.'

'Well, I—'

'But Roger's still hanging round.'

'Roger? I thought he was nice.'

'Yes, very. It's embarrassing. Yech.'

'Oh, a nerd?' Showing she knew the words.

'Sort of.'

'Where'd you go last night?'

Megan bit into the anchovy, tomato and cheese and bobbed her head to give herself time to answer. All the pizza and the good old friend talk were a trap and she should have known better. She watched Mum wrinkle her nose at Walter as she fed him a sliver of pizza, laughter and baby talk, but the house had become cold.

'Well?'

'Just went down to the wharves and sat. Sorry about the drama.'

'That all, Megan?'

'Yes. Just watching the ships.' Megan was surprised that she did not stammer.

'You were alone?'

'I saw Bea.' Does she know something?

'The Cat Lady? You were a long time gone.'

'I was miserable.'

'Don't do it again, Megan. It's dangerous. All right?'

'All right.' Off the hook. Megan began to relax.

'Your father phoned.'

'Oh.' Telling her, or another stage in the trap? Trying to make her forget what she had said?

'Still got his girlfriend. But he wants to see you.'

'I don't want to see him.'

57

One sunny afternoon she had bounced up to her father's cupboard in search for an old tennis racquet. And found it totally bare, as if he had never existed at all. She had found a message in the kitchen and had to phone Mum at the library. Megan could still feel the dead desolation of that afternoon.

'I said you might feel that way,' said Mum softly. 'But you might have to meet him sometime.'

'I don't want to.'

'Well, that's in the future anyway. Eat up. This Roger, is he that bad?'

Between bites Megan talked of Roger, growing her hair long, the basketball team, her chances at the exams, and eventually a phrase or two of Dad. But she watched every word she said.

Megan felt that everything she told her mother was being heard by Kel's Hunters.

9
Tiger

Kel swung his arms about and clapped his hands. 'It's a lot better now. The bruise is still there but it doesn't hurt so much.'

'Good.' Megan was looking at the floor. She tried to sound cheerful, but the effort showed in her voice.

'And this place is great, like a haunted house, with lifts and chutes everywhere. The bales come in on that slide at the roller door, come up here on the old lift and go down there on the wooden rails on the stairs—where you almost fell. And there's other chutes and little lifts to get a bale anywhere. You'll have to see.'

'Yes, good.'

'What's the matter? I haven't transmitted anything at you since yesterday.'

'Maybe you'd better go away.'

'Oh?'

'The men are still looking for you. You'd better get out of here before they catch you.' Megan placed her smuggled food on the bale between them.

Kel looked hurt. 'You don't want me around.'

'What?'

'It's all right. No different at home, really. Dear old Mum's been watching me like I was some sort of snake for months. The old man talks at me but keeps his eyes anywhere else. You get used to it. "Watch out for Kel, he's a Martian."'

'Oh, Kel . . .' Megan jerked her head up and stared at him.

'Might as well go back to Alcatraz.'

'Don't be silly. You can stay here as long you want.'

'You sure?'

'I just don't want you caught.'

'You don't mind me, then.'

'No, I don't mind you. Whatever gave you that idea?'

Not even when I'm talking in your head?

'Yes, I do mind you talking in my head. Stop that!'

'Sorry.' But Kel was almost beaming. 'Maybe you even like me.'

Megan snorted. 'You're getting like Roger.'

'Who's Roger?'

'A pest who keeps on asking me to go around with him.'

'I don't like Roger.'

'It's you I've got to worry about.'

'Me? I'm harmless, a pet mouse.'

'It's getting hard to bring food. Mum is beginning to wonder what I'm doing. Maybe she's talking . . . anyway, she's asking me where I go.'

'On Saturday morning?'

'All the time. And I can't get you fresh clothes. The men that are hunting for you, they are everywhere. They are going to see that this woolstore is

60

open, and there is an old man in the street who is always watching.'

'Always?'

'Almost always. I don't know what he's watching for, but he's out there most of the time and he must've seen me coming in or going out by now. All your hunters have to do is ask him.'

'Why does he do that? Maybe this place is not so good after all.'

'I'll keep on helping, but isn't there somewhere you can go?'

Kel thrust his hands in his pockets and half-turned from Megan. 'I don't want to go . . .'

Megan watched the boy as he sagged his shoulders and blinked at his feet. But she said nothing.

'Well there's always Nan,' Kel said bleakly.

'Who's Nan?'

'Lives out west, on her own. She's an old tribal woman but she understands whatever I've got. I can stay with her.'

'Anywhere's better than here. I saw the men last night outside my house.'

Kel sighed. 'Okay, I go. Can you lend me some money?'

Megan emptied her pockets of a few notes and a heavy pile of coins. 'I emptied my money-box,' she mumbled.

'You knew I'd go, didn't you?'

'Whatever you decided, we needed money.'

Kel relaxed a little. 'Yeah, suppose. After breakfast, you coming to the station, see me off?'

'Oh, yes.'

Kel didn't talk much as he ploughed through the cheese, sausage and apple in Megan's bag, so

61

Megan talked about the Hunters (no, she hadn't seen them today), Mum and, clumsily, Dad.

'Just disappeared? Wish mine had. Both of them. Let's go.'

They stepped between the wooden rails down to the door and peered into the street. The old man was leaning on his gate, apparently staring at them from a hundred metres away.

'What do we do?' hissed Megan.

Kel looked at the man, at the rushing people and crawling cars that filled Dalgleish Street and pushed Megan out of the door. 'Go!'

They walked quickly up the road, ignoring the few puzzled glances from people on the footpath. When they sailed past the old man they didn't even rate a blink. He was staring at the ships in the harbour.

'That was easy,' Kel said smugly.

'I don't think he even sees us. What is he looking at?'

'Who cares? We're safe.'

'You going to write, Kel? I want to hear how you are . . .' Megan said as they turned out of Dalgleish Street and toward the shopping centre.

'To get your money back?'

Megan stopped in the middle of the footpath and her face darkened.

'No, no, sorry, Megan. Didn't mean that at all.'

'Well, watch it, buster. I'll give you my address.'

'Maybe I don't have to write. Keep your head open.'

'You can transmit from the bush?'

'Who knows?' Kel stopped outside a games

arcade and arched an eyebrow. 'Just hang on a minute. Can't resist these.'

'Come on Kel, it's risky.' Megan reached for Kel's arm.

'They don't have these in the bush. Not Nan's bush. Last chance.' Kel twisted into the flashing, roaring, clanging, whining cave.

'Oh, Kel!'

He reached a purple rocket, climbed down into the shiny cage and waved at Megan.

'I'll wait,' Megan muttered. She was beginning to wish she had not bothered to pick the boy up from the bricks. Too much of a burden.

Helmet on, coins in the slot and Kel was flying through the disintegrating universe on the screen before his eyes. 'Yahee!'

Megan stepped clear of the entrance and watched the street for the Hunters' car. Kel didn't deserve to get away, he really didn't.

'You know him, Megan?' Roger was pointing back into the cave, a little sadly. Behind him Hornsey was cheering someone and Little Pam was walking up with a net of oranges. Was everybody here?

'Sort of.' He dances in my head.

'He's a bit of a hot shot.'

A small group was forming round Kel, who was riding his rocket like a cowboy, shouting loudly and gleefully.

'He shows off a bit.'

'A bit! Where d'you know him from, Megan?'

'The swamp,' said Hornsey. 'That's where she gets all her boyfriends. Find a frog and zap, there you are.'

'Shut up Hornsey,' said Megan. She looked over the big girl's shoulder and glimpsed the Hunters' blue car sliding easily toward the shopping centre from two blocks away.

Let him be caught, thought Megan, but she turned from Roger and took a step into the cave.

A solid gasp spread from the kids around Kel's rocket and the sound sucked in almost everyone around the cave. Megan could take two more steps, then she could not move forward, backward or sideways.

Kel was riding his rocket through supernovas, black holes and asteroid storms with his arms folded. And the point totals were tumbling wildly above the screen.

You silly twit, Megan thought and yelled: 'Kel!'

She might as well have whispered. Against the growing din she needed a bomb at least. And the car was no more than a block away.

She waved her arms and shouted again but Kel was destroying an alien fleet.

You'll never get him, never. He's not listening. 'Kel!' Just can't.

Transmit? He can transmit. What'd he say? Just push the thought out?

Kel?

Kel looked up from the screen and his rocket crashed loudly, to the disappointment of the crowd.

Kel, they're coming now.

And the slick men stood on the rim of the crowd, their car stopped in the middle of the road and a finger pointing straight at Kel.

Kel turned back to the screen and the blazing

64

universe began to change. Stars, meteors, planets rushed to the centre of the screen like mice for a hole. They whirled round each other, touched, bubbled, changed colour and shape.

For one moment the screen was filled with a tiger. A tiger, with dripping fangs, glinting and streaked eyes, whiskers rasping against the metal, its breath misting the glass.

Someone gasped. Everyone hushed.

The tiger roared. Roared so loudly the game machines rattled on the floor, a stack of coins slid off a shelf and a distant cat shrieked up a tree.

The crowd turned, shuffled a moment and fled, pushing Roger, Hornsey and the Hunters before them. Megan was struck by a big shouting boy, reeled into the gutter and plucked to her feet by a skinny hand at her elbow.

Thanks Megan, and she was being hauled past the tumbled Hunters, across the road into a lane.

Kel ran with Megan in a great curve across the suburb, down a crowded street, past her house and slowing only as they approached the wreck at Laslo's wall. Adrian's car was buckled and steaming, thrust into Laslo's tiny front garden. Megan stopped beside the car but there was no sign of either Laslo or Adrian, and Kel reached back and pulled her away.

They jogged round the school, under the sky train, along the warehouse and fell inside the woolstore after only the briefest of precautions.

'Poor Laslo, the bend again,' Megan wheezed, and widened her eyes. 'And Adrian! He's got to be hurt, in hospital, even. What happened? Brakes, for sure.'

65

Kel leaned against the stairs.

'Why do they do these things? Fix the engine, forget the brakes; feed the cats, but don't look after yourself; chase a girlfriend and lose your family . . .'

'Megan . . .' said Kel.

'Eh? And you, you're no better. What was that? That tiger in the box—another crummy trick of yours? You could've hurt someone.'

Kel didn't answer. He just studied her face.

'What are you looking at?' Megan felt herself flushing.

'You,' he said quietly. 'You can do it too.'

10

The Nail

Megan frowned. 'What are you saying?'

Kel stabbed the air with his finger. 'You. You were transmitting in that game joint. About as well as me.'

'I was talking to you—transmitting?—when you were stuck in that wrecked house. It wasn't really new, was it?'

Kel shook his head, very hard. 'That was different. I was listening and you were only just getting the words past your nose. This time I wasn't listening at all, and you came through like a cop siren.'

'Oh.' Megan started to smile, then stopped. 'Doesn't matter. What are we going to do with you now? They almost caught you. They know you're close.'

Kel wrinkled his nose and stood up. 'They don't know I'm here. Come on up top.' He pounded up the steps, filling the thin bars of sunlight with glinting specks of dust.

Megan caught him on the first landing. 'They will. People all over the place saw us running.'

Kel wasn't stopping. 'Kids running? Nobody notices that. Kids walking, reading newspapers, maybe, but never running.'

'Oh, very smart. We went past our place and Mum probably saw me. If she didn't, Mrs Gleason did, or somebody in our street did.'

Kel hesitated in his loft, then turned to the rusty iron ladder bolted to a column and a beam. 'To the roof.'

'And Little Pam, Roger, everybody saw me run off with you. The Hunters will ask them where I live, for sure. They will be waiting for me.'

Kel almost ran up the rungs, the drumming of his feet ringing around the woolstore. 'You tell them you just met me and you lost—' Kel pulled on a rusty bolt and heaved against a closed wooden hatch '—me round some corner. Ahh . . .'

The hatch pulled a grey mass of spider webs apart as it creaked away from Kel's hands. Warm air rushed past Kel, stirring dust into an eager chase round Megan's feet.

'I'm not much good at telling lies.'

'Okay, so you don't go back.' Kel heaved himself toward the clear sky and disappeared.

'Oh, that's really bright, that is.' Megan squinted as she climbed the last few steps and swung herself on to the roof. A speck of dust or rust had caught in her right eye and she stopped and wiped both eyes carefully with her handkerchief. She blinked furiously until her eye was flooded clear before she looked around the roof.

For an instant she was standing by the hull of an overturned boat in a rolling sea, with a square-capped funnel rearing from the back of a wave and a small raft behind it. She moved her head, and the rolling sea was the sawtooth roof of the gallery, the ranks of vertical windows glinting below the constant swell of the red-streaked corrugated iron sheets. The hull was the gable roof covering Kel's loft, cutting across the waves of the gallery roof and being pushed against the tall red brick wall of the warehouse. The funnel was a grey air duct with its own small corrugated iron roof and the raft was an odd wooden pallet, too small to be placed under a bale of wool, too big to come through the hatch.

Megan frowned, shrugged and lifted her eyes. The rolling roof was fenced in by ornamental stucco walls and beyond these was a panorama of almost everything. A mosaic of brown, red and silver roofs climbing the slope, the small white square of the pub, the ragged cliff of the shopping centre on top of the hill, the isolated fig tree of the school, the flashing blue of the harbour and the distant city—just today a wizard's castle.

But there was no sign of Kel.

'Kel . . .' she called, quieting her voice from a shout to a whisper even as she opened her mouth.

He's fallen over the edge, that's what he's done.

Megan climbed the nearest sawtooth peak and to the brittle fibro-cement roof over the loft. She walked gingerly toward the rear of the woolstore, looked down, sucked in a breath and shuffled backwards.

On Dalgleish Street the woolstore was only two storeys high, but its rear had been hacked from a sandstone cliff. It dropped more than four storeys to a neglected stone courtyard, roughly at the same level as the wharves. The usually lofty white concrete of the skytrain was now actually below

Megan as it curved toward the water. A solid stanchion slid down, narrowed and spread into the edge of the courtyard. A tree near the stanchion was little more than a straggly weed. The ground was a long way down but Kel was not there.

What did he say? Something about you not going back?

Megan pushed herself from the low wall and looked again at the roof, this time seeing it as a trap.

What do you know about Kel? Nothing, except he can do strange things and some men are looking desperately for him. Maybe they are police after all. Maybe he kills people.

Kel bobbed above the ridge of the loft roof and he grinned. 'What's up?'

'Would you—' Megan started squealing in fright before she regained control of her voice '—stop your silly games!' She hadn't realized she had been that badly affected.

'I'm not playing games.' Kel sounded wounded. He waddled along the ridge toward Megan, tossing a few nails in the air.

Megan walked softly back to the hatch, listening to the fibro-cement move beneath her feet. She was very glad to step down to the solid iron of the sawtooth roof. 'Well, what are you doing?'

'Showing you something.' Kel slid down from the ridge, and skipped over to the wooden pallet. He began to dance on the pallet, shuffling it along the corrugations.

Megan frowned. 'It's a very old roof.'

Kel laughed and soft-shoe shuffled at her. 'This

building likes me. Wouldn't give way, would you?' He clapped his hands and shook his lips about.

'All right, I'm shown.'

'No, you're not. Sit down.' He sprawled beside the pallet and slapped it. 'Wonder what this is doing on the roof, anyway.'

Megan squatted slowly on the edge of the pallet.

Kel looked at her oddly but stood a nail on its point on the wood. Then he withdrew his hand and left the nail standing. 'You asked me how I worked the lock. This is how.'

'It is stuck in the wood,' said Megan, moving up.

Kel blinked. The nail fell. He stared at the nail and it slowly stood up, wrote 'Megan' across the platform and fell again.

'All right, I'm sorry,' Megan said. 'That's great.'

'Now you do it.'

'Come on, Kel. I'm not a wizard. Not in a million years.'

'Neither am I. Try.' Kel pressed the nail into Megan's palm.

Megan placed the point of the nail on the platform and very slowly lifted her fingers from the haft. The nail fell.

'Try again.' Kel guided Megan's fingers back over the nail, and spoke very quietly. 'Now, feel the nail with your mind, until you can sense its weight, the jagged little piece of iron below the head. When you feel it that way, you don't need to feel it with your fingers.'

Megan was beginning to tell Kel what he could do with his experiment when she felt an odd

71

sensation. Something like a hair being drawn across her right temple—from the inside.

'Silly . . .' she murmured, and took her hand away.

The nail wobbled and stood straight.

11
Raffles

For the first wondrous half hour Megan explored the new feeling in her head like a child skating on ice for the first time: at first hovering a touch away from the barrier, then an adventurous toe sliding free for a moment, a nervous retreat, a push from the barrier on both wobbling feet, a desperate scrabble back, and then a short triumphant glide alone on the ice. Megan held the nail upright with a thought, then let it go, rolled it about the platform, lifted it up, let it go, lifted it again, even shimmied it like a tiny rock singer.

Kel sprawled on the roof and laughed. 'Heavy metal, man!'

The nail turned toward him and bounced on its point in tiny fury.

'All right, all right, take it easy. You are getting it.'

Megan let the nail die and roll to one side. 'My head hurts,' she said.

'Yeah, it does when you start. This is the first workout you've ever given that part of your head.'

Megan picked up the nail and rubbed it with her fingers as if she expected it to perform on its own.

'How d'you like it?'

Megan stared at the nail. 'I don't know,' she said slowly. 'It's a bit scary, isn't it? Like dreaming and then finding out that you're not.' She tried a smile, but she looked up and the smile faded from her face. 'But what am I?'

Kel looked up. 'What d'you mean?'

'Nobody does this.' She made the nail somersault on her palm. 'We can do things nobody can. What are we?'

'Martians.' Kel caught the terrified expression on her face and shrugged. 'You're too serious. You're not a Martian.'

'Very funny. I still want to know.'

'And we're not ghosts—I don't think so, are we? You're only Megan, a bad-tempered city kid and I'm Kelaway Rader, a ferret from the bush. We are only using a part of our head the others don't know about yet. That's what Nan told me, when they were all telling me I was a monster. It's natural, she said.'

'But why us?'

'No big deal. What about the ESP people? Give them a photo of a missing person and they can sometimes tell where he is and what happened to him. Some ESP experts are so good the police use them. Just a different part of the head.'

'They aren't police, those men after you, are they?'

Kel almost laughed. 'Thought you were a bit funny before. What, Kel's an axe murderer on the run?'

Megan flushed. It was that silly, wasn't it?

'Well, no, they aren't cops, just goons for the

scientists. Something like truant offices for Alcatraz. They aren't going to catch me—ever.'

'They nearly did.'

'Yeah, I nearly forgot where I was. They won't get that close again. They won't do the Raffles trick on me.'

'Raffles? Oh, the dog—'

'Not just the dog. My mate. They killed him, y'know that? They just killed him.'

Megan placed the nail before her. 'I'm sorry.'

'Doesn't matter. The thing is Raffles knew what they were going to do. Better than they did. He went wild in the cage, bit at them, tried to tell me, but I couldn't understand it. Then the earphones went on. What they said afterwards was that they were trying to work out where Raffle's smartness was. What part of his head made him smarter than they were. So they were using sound to block off parts of his brain, to stop him thinking.'

Kel looked at the nails. They lifted from the pallet and hurtled against the hatch door. Only one fell to the roof.

'And Raffles howled and covered his nose. I was telling them to cut it out and some great twit reached in through the door of the cage to adjust the earphones. Raffles bit him on the hand and went through that door and out of the lab like it was on fire. With the earphones still on, so he couldn't think.

'I hear the big truck's brakes squealing long before Raffles' yelp. The truckie said the dog was just standing in the road, waiting for the truck to hit him.'

Megan groped for the right words to say, then reached forward and squeezed Kel's hand.

'Yeah.' Kel's voice was a little faint and shaky. 'One of the Hunters called Raffles "that stupid freak hound." Then I ran.'

'Yes, I guess we all are.'

Kel lifted his eyes from Megan's hand. 'What?'

'Stupid freak hounds.'

Kel tried a twitch on the side of his mouth. 'Dad called me a bloody gremlin.'

'They call me a witch at school.'

'Really? What about a devil?'

'Black spirit.'

'Necromancer. Really. Mum used it. Means people who talk with the dead.'

'Seer.'

'Beelzebub.'

'Bunyip.'

'Sorcerer.'

'Martian.' And this time both of them were giggling.

'Freak.' Kel sprawled on the tar. 'Hey, hey, that time it didn't hurt at all.'

'That time there were two of us.'

'Yeah, I suppose.' Kel sat up and half-turned from Megan.

'What's wrong?'

'Maybe I shouldn't have taught you that nail trick.' Kel had dropped the giggle like a mask.

'Why?'

'It's not much fun out here, where Raffles and me have been. Maybe it is better to forget about it, leave that part of your head alone.'

'Else I wind up in Alcatraz?'

'That's only a part of it. The parents and me, we might've got along okay sometime, I can't remember now. I can't remember when I had friends, people to talk to without them waiting for you to go weird on them. But I can remember when it all started to go bad, when I ran my bike into a tree and I was seeing two of everything. The Old Man found me, said I kept calling for him, and he was twenty kilometres away.

'If I had stopped then, before I started, it would've been all right, but I was only eight so I had to see what I could do. And every time I was caught doing something people would get real angry and frightened. When I made chalk write on the blackboard I got kept at home and kids would hide when they saw me coming. A couple of nights there were bricks through the windows and Mum tried to pretend I wasn't there. Only person who liked to see me was Nan and maybe that was because she was an outcast too.

'Anyway when I lifted Mum's cat by looking, that was the end of everything. Bang, to the doctor, bang, to the hospital, bang, in come the Hunters with all their forms for Mum and the Old Man to sign, and bang, off to Alcatraz. I was really glad to say good-bye to the family, home, the town—everything. But you don't want to follow me. Let's stop and forget what we've done.'

Megan smiled with a little pain. 'I'm already there.'

'No you're not. What have you done?'

'That teacher, I saw he was going to die . . .'

'Maybe, so some kids call you a witch. They

don't mean it, they still treat you normal. But they will stop treating you normal if you go on. Your family, they will run out on you . . .'

'Dad already has. Don't worry about it.'

'Yeah, well I want you to think about it. I don't want to push you into something where you don't really want to go.'

'Go where? Is there something else?'

'More than moving the nails about? Yes. Alcatraz showed it to me.'

'What, then?'

'What about getting something to eat?'

'You're changing the subject.'

'Yeah. Let's both think about things. Look, I don't know about you, but I am very hungry.'

'You will be here when I come back?'

'Maybe.'

'Oh, so I go down, buy a loaf of bread, cheese and whatever and then I have to eat it all by myself back here.'

Kel passed some of Megan's money back to her, and shrugged. 'Maybe it's better that you don't come back. If I'm still here you might learn how much of a freak you are. 'Bye.'

12
Roger

Megan slid down the ladder from the roof, hardly touching the rungs and took the steps of the woolstore at a run. She was going to grab a pie or something from the shopping centre and bolt back so fast that the ratbag of a boy would have no time to move. And he thought he was frightening her!

Echoes of her footsteps slid into the dark corners of the building and clattered back, chasing her to the door. She forced herself to stop with her hand on the handle, ignored the ghosts still running, and peered up the road, at the few people walking away from her and the old man looking far over her head. She stepped quickly into the sun.

The old man did not move. He really didn't see what he was looking at. She was away in a flash—

'Megan!'

Roger. Coming round a corner at the bottom of the road. Probably saw you coming out from the woolstore. Caught.

Roger smiled and waved at her and she waited on the footpath for him, as still as a cornered cat.

'What're you doing?'

Megan weighed the question. Just a greeting, possibly not an accusation. 'Oh, wasting time.

79

You know.' Tilting her head with a small smile. She walked across the road to draw Roger from the woolstore.

'Yeah, I do it all the time. You know they are going to make it into flats?'

'What?'

'The old building there, the woolstore. It's been sold.'

'Oh. What do you think the old man is looking at?' Anything to change the subject.

'What old man?'

'Him, up ahead. All the time he's leaning on his gatepost, looking down Dalgleish Street at the harbour, and there's nothing there. All the time.'

'Oh, Alfred.'

'You know him?'

'Just to talk to. Sometimes he likes to talk. Been here all his life, 92 years.' Roger suddenly raised his voice. 'Hello Alfred, Megan here wants to know what you're watching.'

'Roger!'

The Old Man of Dalgleish Street swivelled his mottled head like a gate on a rusty hinge, focused his colourless eyes on Megan and dismissed her.

'Clippers,' he said, and returned his gaze to the water.

Roger dipped his head and hustled Megan past. 'He didn't feel like talking. Sorry.'

'Clippers? Clipper ships? There haven't been any clipper ships in Sydney for—oh—almost a century.'

'He knows that.'

'Well, then what is he looking for?'

'He remembers.'

'Oh.' Megan stopped and looked at Roger as if she had only seen a part of him in the past. Roger knew the old man, understood him. How many more mysteries did he know about?

'I forgot,' Roger said. 'Your mum wants to see you.'

Does he speak to everyone in Balin Dock? 'Oh. What for?'

'I dunno. She sounded urgent.'

'I'll see her later.'

'I wouldn't. She looked funny. You done anything?'

'No, no. Probably lost her purse.' Well that's that, anyway. If Kel wants to run he would be off now. Thank you Roger. 'I'll go see her now.'

Megan increased her pace up the hill, but Roger stayed with her. Was he going to follow her through the front door?

'What about the tiger in the games arcade, hey?'

'Tiger?'

'A lot of kids say they saw a tiger in the rocket game. Didn't you see it?'

'A tiger? In the game?' Walking faster. 'No. So what?'

'In the rocket game. It shouldn'a been there. It looked real. Frightened a lot of kids.'

'What, was it in the seat?'

'You were there,' Roger sighed. 'It was in the screen.'

'Oh. A tiger. In the screen.'

'Forget it. Who was the kid? Don't say which kid, the kid you ran off with after the tiger.'

'Oh him. I'm eloping with him.'

'Hah. Har-dee-har-har. Nobody round here ever

81

saw him before. Hornsey reckons the police are after him.'

Megan slowed her pace so suddenly that Roger shot past her. 'Hornsey doesn't know anything. Look, I don't know the kid at all, he pulled me out of the way of that stampede from the game place. He went one way. I went the other. That was it.'

'Sure.'

Okay, so you don't lie well. So what? 'What d'you mean, "sure"? You can believe anything you want.'

'Okay, okay. He just may be bad news. Like Hornsey says. You don't want to take risks.'

'Thanks for worrying about me.' Megan could see her house now and at least there was no blue car parked outside.

'Do I sound like a little old aunt?'

Megan had to smile. 'No, really. That's what friends sound like, isn't it?'

'Suppose. Well . . . look, want to go fishing tomorrow?'

Megan started to shake her head, but stopped with her hand on the gate and said: 'Where?'

'Near the wharves. There's a great spot at the old workshops, jewfish, bream, flathead. Want to try?'

'Oh . . .' Kel's not in the woolstore now, he's not going to be there tomorrow. And who needs any more of his funny magic? How to be a freak. 'Why not?'

Roger's face brightened in surprise. 'Great. Pick you up at seven in the morning. Okay, great.' He turned quickly as if he didn't want to give her time to change her mind.

'Wait, wait. What do I bring?'

'Nothing. Just you. I'll have everything.' Roger ran off.

Megan watched him go and walked to her front door with a small shrug.

Mum opened the door before she reached the knob. She looked haggard, like she did after one of the big brawls with Dad. 'You're all right?' she said and hugged Megan.

'Sure. Why?'

Mum looked back into the house. 'We have a visitor.'

'Hello, Megan, we've met before.' Hunter number one was moving from the shadows of the corridor. 'Come in.'

Give Kel warning. Now! No, wait. 'Hi,' Megan said with a smile.

'I'm Arthur Bennect,' the hunter said sweetly. 'Did Kelaway tell you what I do?'

'Who?' Megan said, quite honestly.

He means Kel and he's setting traps. He's going to catch you.

Bennect kept on staring at Megan while he sat down in the living room. 'You know him, Megan. You were seen running with him in the shopping centre.'

'Oh, him. Is he the one you were looking for before? I feel all goose-pimpley. Was I in danger?' Megan looked sideways at Mum and caught the pressed line of her mouth.

'Where is he, Megan?'

'I don't know, sir.'

'Why don't—'

'He might be in the city now.'

83

'In the city?'

'He was asking me where he could catch the skytrain.'

'Where did you meet him?'

'We didn't really meet. He was playing with one of the computer games in the centre and I was outside and the game went wild or something. Hundreds of kids came running out of the games place and I was knocked over and this boy picked me up and ran with me.'

Bennect stroked his lip. 'And you went with him to the station?'

Trap! That's where the other man is.

'No. He asked me, I told him and he went away.'

'And that was all of it? What did he tell you?'

'Nothing much. Said he went to a special sort of school and he liked dogs.'

'Liked dogs?'

'That's what he said. What did he do?'

'He hasn't done anything, yet. But he's not a normal boy and we must protect him before he gets into terrible trouble. He needs the security of the special school desperately. You understand?'

'I think so. He is mentally ill?'

'Yes, that will do. So, Megan, where is Kelaway now?'

'I'm sorry, but I don't know.'

Bennect sat back in the chair and his face darkened. 'I think you are playing games.'

'I'm sorry—'

'Do you want to see the police?'

'No! I—'

'You can be taken to the police station and interrogated like a common—'

'Enough!' Mum strode between the Hunter and her girl.

'I will not be obstructed—'

'I will not have my daughter threatened in her own home. Out!'

Bennect faltered. 'I did not mean—'

'And I will report this to your superiors. Out, before *I* call the police.'

Bennect went, quietly.

Megan stared at her quivering mother in astonishment. 'You were tremendous. Absolutely.'

Mum looked at Megan uncertainly, then squeezed her and beamed. 'I was, too, wasn't I? The cheek of the man.'

Megan nodded and told herself that she was through with Kel, through with his crummy spy dramas, through telling lies to nasty little men and dragging Mum into the mud, through with walking nails. Through with it all. Time to think only of outfishing Roger the Dull.

'But I'm not doing that too many times,' said Mum and flopped on to the sofa. 'Get me a cup of tea while I stop shaking.'

Megan nodded, slid into the kitchen and put on the jug.

'Sorry about the man, Mum.'

'It's all right. Maybe I'd better really call the police. He's out there terrorising Balin Dock.'

Hope Kel's done what he said he'd do and left. Hope they never catch him.

Megan picked the mug down from the cupboard and tossed in a teabag.

Maybe I'd better warn him anyway. *Kel? You listening? Don't go near the station.*

'S all right. I'm just resting for now.

It really works, doesn't it?

The jug began to bubble and Megan unplugged it. Then she pressed her lips together, placed the jug on the bench and stood back.

The jug lifted unsteadily from the bench moved across the kitchen and slowly poured steaming water into the mug.

'Oh dear,' said Megan.

An hour later she stepped on to the warehouse roof with two large pies and some cheese.

'Now,' she said. 'What sort of a freak am I?'

13
Caterpillar

Kel was sitting on the pallet, looking across the water at the city. 'They pulled this wooden thing up from the street just for a lunch break sunbake,' he said. 'End of mystery. Thought you'd come.'

He smiled slowly at her. His skin was dark and polished in the sinking sun and he might have been carved.

'I almost didn't. One of them was at my place.'

He shrugged. 'You didn't give me away. I knew you wouldn't.' He reached out for one of the pies and attacked it.

'I'm only your food bearer. Yas, massa.'

He looked up from the pie, gravy and tomato sauce smeared above his lip. 'Something wrong?'

'No, what could be wrong? What are we going to do, bend nails?'

Kel stood up with the dripping pie almost stuck to his face. He beckoned to Megan to sit down. 'I'll show you.'

'Tell me first.'

Kel shook his head. 'No. You mightn't believe it.'

'I poured a jug of water. Just by looking at it. I can believe anything.'

'Just sit. Make yourself comfortable.'

Megan sighed, put the remaining pie and the cheese on the pallet and settled beside Kel. She was too close to the dripping mess Kel was making of his pie and wrinkled her nose.

'Now see—what's wrong now?'

'You're terribly messy.'

'That's just too bad. You brung the mess.'

'I'm going to get you properly cleaned up sometime.'

'Going to make a big deal about it, aren't you? I don't ask to be messy. I don't ask to be in this stinking city with nothing and a couple of stupid goons looking for me all the time. You can buzz off.'

'Sorry.'

'No, I've had it, you can just buzz off!'

Megan did not say anything or move a muscle for ten long seconds, then she began to get to her feet.

'Okay,' Kel said.

Megan kept on moving.

'Okay, you can stay.'

'No thank you.'

Kel's eyes widened a fraction. 'Stay. Please.'

Megan stopped. She leaned her head sideways in thought, then eased back to the pallet. 'Just this time,' she said. She picked at the cheese and stared at her feet.

Kel finished the pie and wiped his mouth with the bottom of his shirt. 'Better?'

She shrugged. 'What are we supposed to do?'

'See that weed, the one with the yellow flower right over there?' Kel pointed across the gallery roof, at a flash of green rooted in the shallow gutter below a line of windows. It was twenty metres away.

'Yes. We going to pull it out?'

'Lean back against the air duct, get comfortable. Now keep on looking at the weed and talk with your mouth closed.'

'You mean mumble.'

Just keep on looking hard.

'Oh, that.' *Why?*

Because this is the only way we can do it.

Do what?

Look at the flower. Look at the spikey yellow petals.

You're kidding! I can hardly see the flower.

Try.

Megan squinted at the yellow spark dancing against a grey window until her eyes hurt. This was stupid, a waste of time and the wood was too hot to sit on.

Relax. Don't stop. Just relax.

What I'll do is go to sleep and he can worry about weeds.

But after a while the hot hard wood of the pallet and its sideways angle stopped worrying Megan and yes, she could see the needles that made up the ball of the flower. Only just.

I can see them. Now what?

What about the caterpillar climbing the stalk?

Come on· . . . oh, yes.

And the caterpillar's eye?

Yes . . . yes, I can!

Megan could see trees of grass, huge blades of dusty green clattering at each other round an eruption of yellow fire, reflecting the dying sun. A black-snouted creature lifted its head to stare at the sky while the rear of its long, long body marched calmly to catch up. The creature's purple-blue eye swivelled toward Megan and two pincers chopped hungrily at a blade before it.

You there? Yes, you are. How d'you feel?

Megan stared at the caterpillar, big as a goods train, and heard the patient grinding of its pincers as it moved.

I'm scared. You shrunk us, or something?

Nothing like that. We're just looking.

Megan felt a powerful force pulling at her back, as if she was wearing a metal suit near a huge magnet. The caterpillar began to shrink and the yellow fire became a flower again . . .

Come back!

She fought the magnet until she was almost touching the caterpillar's right eye. The caterpillar didn't seem to be bothered, but Megan recoiled from the glinting hairs on its head and bobbed back a little. She could still reach out and touch one of the marching legs.

But with what?

Megan suddenly realized that she had no hands, no feet, no legs, nothing at all. She looked around in panic, but there was nothing but the munching caterpillar and the flower.

Where are you? She was almost shouting.

Hey, hey, take it easy. I'm right beside you.

I can't see you. I can't see me!

Okay, it's all right. Look back. All the way.

Megan floated her eyes from the caterpillar, as if she was drifting on a raft. A massive blade of grass swayed before her and slid sideways. A broad river flowed between cliffs of glass and a red-cresting ocean to a tilting wooden island and two huge, distant feet.

Hers.

Megan lifted her eyes and looked from the massive weed across the woolstore roof at Megan. A long-limbed girl with straggly brown hair in a pair of frayed jeans and a T-shirt, sitting beside a dark boy with a wide nose and a drowsy look. Neither of them moved a muscle, as if they weren't people at all, just dummies thrown down on the pallet and left staring. Megan stared at Megan, and Megan stared at Megan.

What—

And the magnet grabbed Megan between the eyes, yanked her from the weed and the caterpillar and hurled her along the river-gutter at the Megan sagging against the roof.

Both of them gasped at the impact.

14

Ancient Secrets

Kel grinned at Megan. 'How did you like the journey?'

Megan sat up and rolled her right hand before her, inspecting it very carefully. 'What happened?'

'Just a bit of Remote Viewing. Only it wasn't really remote, was it?'

Megan pulled herself unsteadily to her feet and walked along the gutter to the weed, now a small, unimportant growth on a tiny patch of dirt. She bent over, moved a blade of grass and found the caterpillar. 'I can hardly see it, even from here!'

'That's what the clowns at Alcatraz are carrying on about. I did it the first time just before they got Raffles. A measured kilometre to read the writing on a postage stamp, and they got me to read round corners too.'

Megan sat down heavily. 'What did you say, "Remote Viewing"? What's it mean? That scares me.'

'You saw, didn't—'

'I looked back and I saw me. I was out of my body and I didn't know how to get back in.'

'No worries. Your body pulls you in. You can feel it. Didn't you?'

Megan remembered the magnet, yanking her across space. 'I suppose so.' She closed her eyes, running through the sensations, tasting them for a second time.

'I knew about this before,' Kel murmured. 'I just didn't believe it. When I was hiding out from the parents and just about the whole town, Nan found me and started "demonstering" me. Anyway, she told me about a tribal elder who flew.'

The flower getting slowly bigger, the caterpillar appearing, the caterpillar's eye . . .

'An American astronaut was at a post in the Australian desert just to talk to another astronaut, John Glenn, as he orbited overhead. Some aborigines asked the astronaut what he did. He said he flew among the stars. Ah, say the aborigines, like the elder.'

And turning, slowly, to see a watching stranger. You . . .

'The elder says he'd better go up and see how the other astronaut is getting on.'

And being sucked into yourself. Not that bad. Really.

'And then John Glenn goes overhead in space and he's talking about going through a bunch of butterflies. Nan says the elder was probably up there.'

No worse—no, better—than a roller-coaster.

Megan looked back and looked up at the darkening sky. 'That is a long way up.'

'Do you believe it?'

'I don't know. I wouldn't have believed the pouring jug before this afternoon. And that caterpillar thing . . .' Megan shook her head. 'How long is this Remote Viewing?'

Kel picked some grit from his knee. 'I don't know. I've only done the kilometre. A couple of the scientists were talking about crazy things, but they wouldn't know.'

'What did they say?'

Kel rested his head on the wall and looked at the same stretch of sky as Megan, a moon like a pie-crust and a single bright star in the deep blue.

'See the star?'

'Yes.'

'It's Sirius, the brightest star we've got and it's not a star, it's two. A binary. My crazy scientists say that we didn't know that until 1862 when an American used the world's biggest telescope on Sirius. There is a white dwarf—real heavy star, but only tiny—orbiting the big Sirius and we only photographed it in 1970. That's what they say.'

'Yes?'

'They say that there are some tribes in northern Africa called the Dogon, still pretty primitive, that seem to have known the secret of Sirius for thousands of years. They can draw the oval course of the little star round the big star and they say the little star is heavier than all the iron in Earth. That's pretty right for just a hunk of a white dwarf star.'

'You think they have been out there?' Megan watched the clear, bright light of Sirius, and it chilled her.

'Well, there's only three ways the Dogon could have known about little Sirius. They could have looked through a huge telescope about the time the Pyramids were being built. Like catching a morning bus to Mars—now. Or they could have been told what's out there by a flying saucer . . .'

Megan giggled.

'Well the Dogon think it was flying saucer men, men with fishy tails from Sirius, that told their ancestors everything.'

'Oh.'

'Except some ancient Maoris knew that Saturn has rings, and some pygmies even knew that Saturn has nine moons—a tenth moon was so small it wasn't found until 1966. And not so long ago two men saw blue ice-crystals on Jupiter and a helium tail streaming from Mercury before those things were found by the Mariner 10 probe. None of them knew anything about flying saucers.'

'And the third way is us,' Megan said softly. She saw the hairs on her arms rise and rubbed at them.

'Yeah. Just like us. A Maori resting in his big ocean canoe staring at Saturn and taking off . . .'

'Or a pygmy lying on a rock and whizzing round Saturn, counting moons . . .'

'Or a Dogon elder coming back from his tenth trip to Sirius.'

Kel and Megan stared in silence at the star for a long time.

'You haven't been up there yet?' said Megan slowly.

'Only the kilometre down the road.'

'Why?'

'I wasn't going to do it for them. The dog killers.'

'But now?'

'Now? It's different.' Kel rigidly looked away from Megan. 'You want to?'

95

'I suppose we'd better.' Megan was horrified at the words that were stumbling from her lips. But she could not stop now. 'While we're here.'

'To see if it's all true.'

'To see if we can do it.'

'It'd be great.'

'It would be safe, wouldn't it?'

'Sure. Safe as houses. We are only looking at things, aren't we?'

'That caterpillar couldn't have bitten me, could it?'

'No. You weren't there. You were here, looking there.'

'How far away is Sirius?'

'I don't know. About nine light years, trillions of kilometres.'

'It's too far. I'm not going there.'

'What's the difference? We're just looking.'

'It's too far.'

'All right.' Kel lifted his eyes from the blazing star to the yellow pie-crust. 'What about the moon, then?'

Megan took a long breath as she realized that they weren't kidding any more. What she said now could determine the rest of her life.

'Okay,' she said.

15
Dusty Sea

'All right. Let's go,' said Kel.

'Just like that?'

'Yes. Why not?'

'Well . . . we're not just going to the corner shop, are we? We're going to the Moon, for heaven's sake!'

'So?'

'"So?" That's all you can say? You're hopeless, Kel!' Megan flicked her fingers at him in an angry, frustrated gesture.

The cheese beside Megan wobbled into the air and drifted under her nose.

'Have a nibble. We'll take some cheese to the Moon,' said Kel.

Megan had to smile. She took a small fragment but found herself unable to swallow. 'I suppose we'd better go,' she said. Before I'm too scared to go anywhere.

For a moment Kel was quiet and when he said, 'Yes,' he sounded a little subdued.

Perhaps we shouldn't do it. 'Kel?'

But Kel came back, bright and a little wild. 'Right, kid? Aim for the middle.'

'What middle? Middle of the Moon?'

I'm off! Catch me!
Wait . . .

Megan felt the corrugations of the slanting roof pressing into her back for a long moment. Then she was staring at the warm yellow disc in the deep blue sky, at the fat shadow across the disc, at the smooth seas and the splattering of the craters. And now she was moving.

The warehouse wall at the corner of her eye disappeared, the blue sky became black with a sudden explosion of clear, bright stars. The Moon began to grow before her, swelling like a party balloon. Near the top of the balloon there was a vast crater surrounded by impact streaks, and it wasn't a balloon any more. The Moon was now an orange, with its stem pulled out.

Keep your eye on where we're going, or we're going to wander.

Megan noticed she was drifting towards the giant crater, and flicked her eyes down to the ragged peninsular of smaller craters in the centre of the Moon. Now she could not see anything but Moon.

I'm cold, she complained.

You're not. You just think you are.

Thank you very much. Where are we going?

What about the Sea of Serenity? The Yanks have been near there.

Where?

Down and left from the craters ahead. The big round smooth bit.

Megan moved her eyes to a grey streaked area, rimmed on one side by scarred ranges and clusters of craters. On the other side, a huge breaker, a tidal wave, stretched far across the sea. A lone crater broke the dark surface far behind the breaker.

You mean the sea with the big wave. Looks like someone's head?

Oh, yes. The long rock ridge. Yes, that's the Sea of Serenity.

Megan felt a little embarrassed. *Some sea! It's only rock*, she projected, to make sure Kel didn't think she was an idiot girl.

Lava. But it looks like a sea back on Earth, so it's a sea. Sea of Serenity, Sea of Crisis, Ocean of Storms, Bay of Dew—

How do you stop this thing? Megan was suddenly rushing toward a small crater that had risen from a flat map to something with cliffs and hollows. Other craters were fleeing from her sight.

Oh. I dunno.

You don't know. Help! The crater reared from the grey plain and Megan was going to plough into its rim, one more meteorite.

Look away?

Megan stared in horrified fascination at the dark seam where she was going to hit, watching it open like a rocky mouth—and stopped.

Hah! She felt a surge of relief and moved her eyes to bring her slowly down to the Moon. She felt the magnet at her back, a little weaker, perhaps, but reassuringly there.

You all right?

Yes. Don't look away. Focus your eyes and it stops.

Too late. I sailed off. Where are you?

Megan preened a little. *Oh, I'm on the Moon.*

Oh great. It's a big place, you know?

I'm floating above a little crater near some big craters at the edge of your silly sea.

Never mind. I'll come down and find you.

Don't know how. You can't see me, can you?

I'll find where you're at.

Megan looked about her, at the isolated outcrops of lemon rock, the slanting cliffs of her crater, the distant rock ridge sweeping away with the curve of the Moon, at the rolling, pocked mountains of the sea shore. The Sea of Serenity was now no more than a desert plain, marked by thrown boulders and shadows.

I don't think much of this Moon . . .

Hey, hey, come here!

Where's 'here'?

Oh, try west, near the big crater. You can't miss us.

Us?

Come on, come on!

Megan lifted from the rim of her crater, glanced sideways at a mountain wall thrown up by the impact of a large meteor and scudded across the plain. She lowered her eyes to slow herself and began to sweep from side to side, looking for something, anything apart from the rocks and the dust.

Us?

She slid over the mountain wall to see that the wall formed an almost complete circle round a small plain with a deep hollow, but there was nothing else in the crater. She moved out across a mountain range that echoed the arc of the crater, then a confusion of hills and ridges tumbling towards the sea.

100

There is nothing at all here, she thought. He's playing tricks.

She was drifting out of a short valley when she saw a small and angular shape to her right and leapt her eyes sideways to catch it. Looking like a beach holiday camp, rocks instead of sand, dust instead of water.

You found us. I can tell.

What is it?

Have a look.

There was a tent, a gold tent, no, no, the 'tent's' guy ropes were metal legs and a ladder to the roof. Except the roof was blackened, as if a bonfire had been lit there. There was a spidery jeep with an umbrella parked in front of the tent, except the umbrella was too small, curved up instead of down, and was shiny metal. There was a stiff United States flag on a rod clear of the jeep, and there were many footprints wandering around the site.

Lunar mission? Megan drifted over the burnt-out shell of the landing motor in growing fascination. It really was covered in gold. Gold foil, as if it was a Christmas present.

Apollo. I think Apollo 17, the last. Landed here in 1972, beetled about in their lunar rover, collected a few rocks and blasted off for their orbiter and home.

Megan was hovering above a fine print of a ripple-sole boot in the gravel. *That old? That's almost thirty years ago. It can't be.*

Because of the footprints? No air up here, no wind. It will stay like this until a meteorite hits it. Or until the Yanks come back.

Megan was turning to read the writing on the

101

rocket engine when she was jerked thirty metres from the surface. *The magnet! It wants me . . .*

That's all right. See you down there.

Megan relaxed and she was whipped into space like a fish on the end of a line. The remains of the lunar module and the lunar rover disappeared near the hump of the low mountain as a crater and stretch of sea swam into her vision. She tried to turn, to see the approaching Earth, but the pull was too strong and too fast. The rim of the Moon touched the outer corners of her eyes. The crater that made it an orange swept back. For a moment the Moon looked like a pancake thrown into the sky, then a pie-crust and the hard corrugations of the roof were pushing into her back.

She squeezed her eyes shut, holding the bright image of the huge Moon against her eyelids for a few seconds. She was still soaring through space when she heard the whine of a mosquito and someone shouting in the street below. She sighed and reluctantly opened her eyes.

But Kel had not returned. He was still staring at the Moon, his mouth sagging open as if his mind had curled up and died.

Megan reached for him in fright, then stopped with her hands hovering over his shoulders.

You don't know what you are doing. Stop.

You've got to do something. He's dying or something.

Then Kel blinked and grinned. 'Wow. That was great. Unbelievable.'

'You all right?'

Kel stretched and leapt to his feet. 'Sure. Why? That was fantastic. Wasn't it?'

Megan frowned at Kel, watching him prance about, then smiled. 'Yes, it was. I'll never forget it.'

'Forget it? Ah, that's peanuts. Know what we are? Astronauts. The real thing. Voyagers to the stars.' He suddenly began laughing.

'What's up?' Megan was laughing again.

'The Ruskies and the Yanks, they spend billions of dollars to get to the Moon. We do it on a nibble of cheese.'

'But they can bring back rocks.'

'Yeah, yeah. And they can drive that whizzy jeep up there, wish I could've. But we can see things they can't. Oh, if only they knew!'

'But Alcatraz has got the idea. That's why they are after you.'

'You know, you are a miserable wet blanket. We go to the Moon and all you can think of is the Hunters.'

'Sorry.'

'They've only got an idea it can be done. That's all. They're not sure about it and some of them don't believe anything. Well, I'm not going to tell them and they aren't going to catch me.'

'If you are very careful. You will have to leave here.'

Kel nodded. 'You're right.'

'It's best.'

'I'll leave after tomorrow night.'

'Why then?'

'We've got to do it again. We've got to do a biggie.'

'Oh.' Megan was remembering Kel staring at

103

the Moon with his jaw slack. 'Do you think we should?'

'Come on. We're astronauts, we've got to be up there.'

Megan looked up at the Moon and breathed deeply. 'Yes,' she said. 'We've got to do it again.'

'Tomorrow night,' said Kel.

16
Fishing

Megan was scudding smoothly over a Moon mountain when the mountain began to rock. She rolled in flight, flailed her arms and scraped her nose on a rock . . .

'Come on, Tumblehead . . .'

Who's Tumblehead? . . . and crashed.

Megan opened an eye and looked up at Mum, a soft shape ringed with hazy sunlight. 'Hello.'

'Hello, yourself. You have a gentleman waiting for you.'

'Dad?' A little alarm.

'Roger. Come on, you were supposed to be up and ready to go.'

'What's the time?'

'Quarter past seven. You didn't tell me you were whale chasing, I could have got you up. Now hurry.'

Megan rolled out of bed, thought of telling Roger to go and chase himself, decided against it and raced for the shower. Strange, but she couldn't get rid of the idea that she was covered in Moondust.

'Sorry, Rog,' she said, adjusting a button on her shirt.

'That's all right. No hurry. You want to have breakfast before we go.'

Megan glanced at Mum and shook her head. 'No, I'm not hungry. Let's go.'

They walked down Bates Street as Adrian Thomas kicked sadly at his wrecked car, a sagging, blind machine with the bonnet rearing before the shattered windscreen and a toppling front wheel.

'Were you hurt?' said Megan.

'Wasn't even in it. Two kids pinched it for a joy ride. What's the use?'

'Oh. Sorry, Adrian.'

They walked past Peter Chow and Rosalind Fahed looking at the flats to let ads in the paper, and they talked of them, Adrian's car, fish, lunch and school. They stopped in the sun of Victor Street and listened to Judy plucking out a new song while Laslo mixed a barrowful of cement beside her.

''Allo Megan,' said Laslo. 'I am building a better wall.'

'Hi, Roger,' said Judy. 'I am making a better song about him building the better wall.'

And they all laughed. The Moon seemed a long way away and long ago.

Roger led Megan past the school, between the corrugated iron of the old workshops, and to the worn wooden walkway looking over the still inlet. He baited the lines and relaxed against a creaking post, the bright water playing over his face. Megan sat beside him and did absolutely nothing for a very long time, which was exactly what she wanted.

'No fish,' Roger said, once.

'No,' Megan said later.

'Sorry.'

'Who needs fish anyway?' Megan was looking across the water at a dark sailor slowly painting patches of orange on the hull of his ancient freighter. Above him comforting puffs of white cloud drifted across a gentle blue sky. She wanted it all to stop right here.

'Sorry you came?'

'No.' And Megan meant it. Roger, when you came to think of it, was an easy person to have around. Sort of like an old dog. After Kel he was a holiday. After Kel anyone was a holiday.

Roger glanced over his shoulder, smiled and waved. 'Pam,' he explained.

Megan looked at the tiny waving figure on a bend of the road a hundred metres away. 'You have good eyes,' she said.

'Like a hawk.'

Megan looked up at the sky and smiled.

'What're you doing when you leave school?' asked Roger.

'That's a long way away. I don't have to think about that for years and years.'

'Yeah, that's the best way.'

'Tell you what I'm *not* going to be. A head librarian.'

'Why?'

'You want to see Mum after a bad day. Old bags trying to get out of paying fines for late books, mothers trying to get her to do their lazy kid's project for him, horrible women trying to get books banned, kids drawing moustaches on pictures. So she comes home and takes it out on the rest of us.'

'That's tough. Especially since . . .' Roger petered out.

'Since?'

'You know. Your dad.'

'Oh yes, since. Is there anyone at all who doesn't know?'

'Suppose not. Shouldn'a mentioned it.'

'Doesn't matter. What are *you* going to do when you leave school?'

'Oh.' Roger pulled his line from the water. No fish, no bait, just a streamer of seaweed. 'Be a fisherman.'

They laughed.

'Watcha doing?' Pam was standing behind them.

'Fishing,' said Megan.

'Sort of.'

'Yech.'

'It's all right,' Roger said. 'We never catch anything.'

'But what if you do?' Pam looked horrified.

'We pull it out of the water,' said Megan gently. 'Then we put a foot on it and lever the hook out of the mouth. That is sometimes hard to do, so we have to cut it from the fish's mouth. See Roger's big knife? Then we have to get the guts—'

'Meg . . .' Roger shook his head.

'You are crude,' Pam said, a little faintly. 'I just came over, Roger, about the play tonight.'

'Oh, sure.'

'At St Ignat's at eight. That all right?'

'I'll be there.'

108

'Great. See you. Happy fishing, Meg.' And Pam was gone.

Megan turned to Roger with new interest. 'Play? What play? You an actor, Roger?'

'Sort of. Amateur thing. Pam's dad is directing *The Iron Butterfly* and he needs a pretty stupid admiral's son in a couple of short scenes. So Pam asked me.'

'I didn't know about that. You're really secretive, Roger.'

'Sorry. It's only a little thing. Nothing like Pam on TV. I didn't know anybody was interested.'

'When is your show on? I want to see it.'

'No, don't! It's going to be terrible. I'm going to be terrible.'

'Good. Then I'll blackmail you. You'll never be able to call me a witch again.'

'I never have called you a witch.'

'No, you never have.' Megan let her face fall into a grin. 'And you'd better not. Otherwise I'll zap you to the Moon.'

'Yes sir.'

That easy. You can joke again, you don't have to drive old friends away with fishy gore, out-mean Hornsey, treat Roger like the top nerd of Balin Dock. Probably is, but he's a nice nerd.

Megan eased back on the walkway and thought a bit. She sat in the sun and picked up the strange things that were happening to her, examined them carefully, turned them over, held them up to the light and put them away. While she watched the still water before her she could wonder about what she had seen on the Moon last night, and not be

109

frightened. She could still picture Mum hissing across the table, 'Whyn't you go with him, eh?' But now she could remember Mum before the day Dad disappeared, not quite a barrel of fun but you knew where you stood. And maybe it was getting better. Mum had been great in standing up to Kel's Hunter.

Suddenly Megan looked up at a distant sandy-haired man walking towards her on the road. She gasped and scrambled to her feet.

'Dad?' she whispered. Her eyes brightened, a smile split her face, she arched her body as if she was about to leap at the man.

Roger looked up and frowned.

And the man turned away up a side street.

Megan sagged. 'Not Dad,' she said to Roger, and shrugged. She sat down heavily.

And that was ridiculous. You don't want him now, do you? No, and Mum doesn't want him now. Not since he left. Good for a few laughs, fun to camp with, fix broken things, but that's all gone. Finish. No matter if you never see him again.

'You all right?' Roger was leaning towards her.

'Sure. Why shouldn't I be?' Her voice was catching on something.

'Ah—nothing. Just you look funny.'

'I'm fine,' she said angrily. She whipped her arm across her eyes.

'Okay.'

She pulled her line in, inspected it and threw it out again. 'You know, he had me thinking he left because of something I did. Can you believe that?'

Roger nodded.

'Didn't want to talk about it to anyone. And Mum, I guess she had the miseries too. But we're getting out of it now . . .'

Megan and Roger fished in silence for a while, then Roger pulled in his hook and prepared to throw it out wide. He held the hook in his hand and looked across the water.

'Not my business Meg.'

'What is? Dad?'

'All of it. But this kid, he's getting you in trouble.'

'What kid?'

'They're watching you.' Roger nodded at a near wharf, where two men were standing beside a polished blue car.

Megan sighed. 'They just won't give up, will they?'

'They were asking a lot about the kid at the games arcade. What did he do?'

'Nothing really. He can do something they can't. That's all.'

'And you know what it is? You sound in real deep.'

Megan laughed. 'It's all right, Rog. No crime, nothing to worry about, and after tonight it'll be over. Hey! I've got something!'

17
Ice Rings

Mum looked up from her chair in the sitting room. 'You're going out a lot lately.' She sounded tense.

Megan stopped in the corridor and shrugged. 'I just want to see Roger ham it up. He's in a play.'

Mum relaxed a little. 'I didn't know that. Is he picking you up?'

'He's only down the road at St Ignat's. I'm late. See you.' Megan rushed for the door.

'Be care—'

And she was out and running for the gate. She was astonished at the ease with which she lied now, as if she had been lying all her life. She did not like the feeling.

She ran past the Faheds and the Chows—all of them—arguing angrily on the twilight footpath but looked back at them as she reached Dalgleish Street. Funny, Mrs Fahed seemed to be on the side of Mr and Mrs Chow, shouting at Rosalind and Peter. There was always something new.

Megan was so curious about the row in Bates Street that she almost missed the shiny blue car parked in the shadows fifty metres ahead.

She stopped at the corner.

They won't let go. They are going to keep

following until they catch Kel. Send a message to Kel? He can leave the woolstore while you lead them the wrong way.

Megan leaned on her mind, but then shook her head.

No, that way they win. Why should people like them push us round all the time? We don't do things just because they want us to. We don't stop doing things just because they want us to. Not any more, we don't.

Megan could hear the anger of Peter Chow carry in the warm night air and remembered her own on the waterfront a few hours ago. She turned up Dalgleish Street, not down. She could just hear the low murmur of the car far behind her as she reached Rook Lane and strolled into its shadows. Behind her the car stopped a few seconds, then moved on.

The Hunters would now do the block and be waiting for her at the other end.

Megan ran back to the beginning of Rook Lane and checked carefully that the blue car had left Dalgleish Street.

'Good-bye,' she said with grim satisfaction.

She hared down the hill, crossing Bates Street, slowing only when she had passed the ruined house and was approaching the old man.

'Hello Alfred,' she said. But Alfred merely nodded and kept gazing at the lights of the harbour.

She moved to the woolstore, looked back at the old man for a minute of increasing tension, then shrugged and slid inside.

Kel was on the roof, leaning on the slope of the

saw-tooth and looking bleakly down on the street. 'What's he looking at? The old bloke.'

'Nothing. He—um—pretends this is about 90 years ago and he can see clipper ships in the harbour and bullock drays in the street.'

'For real?'

'Must be sad, trying to see things that don't exist any more.'

'Yeh. If he could only see what we see. Hey! Got any food?' Kel sounded a little artificial.

'You're lucky I'm here at all. They're following me now. They know I've been seeing you.'

'I finished the cheese for breakfast. I've been hungry all day.'

'You want me to get you something? Go down to the shop? 'Course the Hunters will see me and follow me.'

Kel clicked his tongue. 'All right. We've got to go, haven't we?'

Megan looked up, beyond the tall brick wall, beyond the haze of street lights at the Moon and the fine spray of stars beyond. She wasn't frightened any more. Just a little nervous.

'It's a good night.' Kel slid down to the platform and sprawled beside Megan. 'Our last flight. Tomorrow I'm going to shake the city, and the Hunters and hide in the bush.' For a moment he looked unhappy, as if a mask had slipped.

'Anything wrong?'

'Nah. Just a mood.'

'Oh.'

'Just a bit lonely back there. In the bush.'

'There's Nan.'

'No. Not any more.'

'What's happened?'

'Dunno. Can't reach her, can't feel she's there any more. I think she's gone.'

Megan was quiet for a moment. 'You can't be sure. Not from here.'

Kel shrugged and banged his fist on the platform. 'Ah, she's a silly old woman. Forget about her. We've got to go!'

Megan tried to match his sudden brightness. 'Right, yes. Where are we going?'

Kel swept his arm past the Moon and stabbed at a steady prick of white light just clear of the Milky Way. 'There.'

'That's a star. That's too far away.'

'That's a planet, not too far away.'

'Which one?'

'You'll see. Let's go.'

'Oh, all right. Just one thing.'

'Yes?'

'Sorry I was so mean before.'

Come on, I'm off.

Megan glanced sideways at Kel. The boy was slumped back against the corrugated iron, his hands flung wide and his eyes staring at the sky. He looked like a discarded teddy bear.

He's left me, Megan thought in sudden fright. She hunted for the white speck over her head, found it and leaned back against the slope.

Where are you? Kel sounded far, far away.

I'm coming. Wait for me.

It was easy this time, as if she had taken a great stride into the stars with no more effort than a step over a pavement crack. The wall disappeared, the Moon swept out of sight and the stars sprayed out before her, as if a stone had been dropped into a starlit pool. Ahead the white speck became a block, then a tiny head wearing a rakish hat.

Saturn?

Oh, good, you're on the way. I'm there already.

Well, isn't that peaches for you. Megan snapped back. Back to normal.

What's with you?

Megan was about to reply, but the man in the hat had grown and she forgot what she was going to think at Kel.

The head was now a silver ball with a canted disc throwing a sharp shadow across its surface. Saturn was hanging silently in space, now beginning to feel like a planet.

Megan felt something rolling around in her head, a marble trying to find a way out.

What is this? Stop it!

Sorry, I can't help it.

What are you doing?

Now the silver sheen of the planet had broken into stripes of brown and white, the tiger planet, as it grew from a pea to a grape, to an orange, to a pumpkin.

I'm just laughing. I'm having a bath in Saturn's rings, watching snowballs chase icebergs past my nose. Crazy.

Don't get lost.

There were many rings now: white rings, blue rings, green rings and rings of nothing. You could see stars through some of the misty rings and you could see the bottom of Saturn through the space between a bright white ring and a dark blue ring. And now you could see some of the moons. Not

116

like the scarred disc of the Moon as seen from Earth but hard round balls under and above the rings. One moon was rolling around one of Saturn's white belts, seemingly almost touching the planet but throwing a shadow across a ring.

Well, what do you think of it?

For a moment the rings were cut, as if someone had taken a great slice of them and thrown it away. Megan was puzzled and turned to see the distant blaze of the sun, smaller than she had known it, whiter but brighter. She turned back and saw that the rings were continuing, darker, through the slice. She was simply seeing the shadow of Saturn on its rings.

It's fantastic.

Naturally. When I take you on a tour it's the best tour out, and Saturn has got to be the best planet out.

Been to Jupiter?

Nah, haven't been anywhere before you, you know that. We'll do Jupiter next.

The brown and white bands of the planet now filled the sky, huge clouds slowly swirling round the equator. The rings almost touched the eye.

You know we can't do that. You must leave the city.

Oh, yes. I suppose.

I'm at the rings. Where are you?

Silence. Megan slowed herself and stopped just above the rings, almost close enough to hear the white and blue streaks of light flashing past.

Come on, I'm here. Where are you?

Oh, yes. I'm in the ring. Just go the way the ring is going. You'll like it.

Megan sighed but skated above her ring. She speeded up and watched the streaks slow to tum-

117

bling snowballs and ice boulders, then everything seemed to be floating in an almost motionless sea. The ice fragments below Megan were quite still, but the rings nearer the planet were sliding past, like an ocean liner leaving port. A massive block of green ice with a streak of black was drifting immediately beneath Megan so she imagined herself sitting on it.

She was amazed at the sensation and felt herself laughing. This was just the greatest merry-go-round in the universe, that's all!

Like it?

The magnet snatched at her back and Megan broke away, plunging into the ring's frozen storm and out the other side.

Like it? I could stay here for a week and chase icebergs. Better than playing those silly videos, better than winning basketball for a month. How do you feel?

Something like that. Like I'm a king or an emperor. Better than that.

Well, no king had a huge planet like this to play with.

Yes . . .

Yes, what?

Let's not go back.

18
Megan's Star

Megan stopped seeing pictures in Saturn clouds.
*What? You are being silly. You want to stay out here
for ever?*

I didn't mean that at all, tadpole—aweaigh!

You all right? What happened?

*Went through a big hunk of ice. First time I've seen
out from the centre of an iceberg. It's cold. Where was I?*

You want to be another moon of Saturn.

No I don't. But look behind you.

Megan lifted her eyes from the rings, from the
bands of the planet and turned to look at the stars.
They were many, far more than the thousands she
had seen from the city, far more than she had seen
from a country hill on a cold, clear night.

Now they were in their millions, the fine spray
of the heart of the galaxy thinning out to black
chasms in the distant corners of the sky. But the
chasms were not entirely black; there were tiny
pricks even there, if you looked hard enough. The
stars were everywhere and the big ones, the bright
ones, were as different from each other as faces in
a crowd. Here was a large blue star, there a
glowing yellow spark, a rested red giant, a white
hot beacon, and there a pulsar, a star flashing its

lonely distress. Megan felt she could reach out in the shining black and touch all of them.

Pick a star, Kel said.

There's so many of them . . . Why?

Why not? We're out here, but we don't have to go back yet. We can move out from Saturn and see what we can find in our galaxy.

Can we? Do we have the time? Can we change the place we aim for just like that? Is it safe?

The Dogon people got out and saw Sirius and here we are at Saturn, only a planet. This is our only chance to reach a star before I have to go back and start hiding. Pick a star, Meg, and we'll go there.

Megan moved her sight across the galaxy and worried. They had nosed a footprint on the Moon and swum in the rings of Saturn. But the stars, they were different. They were light years away and what is a light year anyway? Surely they had done enough.

Come on, Meg.

Megan took a deep breath and looked at a close cluster of stars in the Milky Way.

All right. The blue star near the five little ones.

Where? There's a lot of blue stars . . .

Saturn's rings are almost pointing at it. Further from the Sun.

Oh, yes. Near the big red one?

That's it.

Right.

Right.

Then here we go.

Well . . .

The rings of Saturn slid aside and were gone. A cold planet rolled like a marble far beneath

120

Megan—Uranus, Neptune?—and she was alone with the stars. And the stars began to move. Some glided to the corners of her eyes, some arched overhead, or skidded from her. One small white star grew rapidly, and split into two white stars. And some stars were too far away to move at all.

Ha! Kel's thought was so close Megan could almost hear him. It was comforting to know that he had not gone off after another star by mistake.

Ha, yourself . . .

Was just thinking. Now we're astronauts, real astronauts. We can tell them all what it's like. What it's going to be like for them.

The stars were getting thicker. Megan passed by one star close enough to call it a sun, round as a cherry, flaring in the dark and with the shadow of an immense planet silhouetted against the fire.

No, I guess not. Kel's thought felt a little sad.

What's wrong?

We can't tell them anything about this, Meg, that's all. Tell them what it's like to chase icebergs round Saturn, and they'll never let us out of Alcatraz. Never. This has got to be just for us.

Ahead the blue star was forming into a pinhead beneath a carelessly flung loop of purple gas.

It's a long way away, Megan said.

Bigger, too. A lot bigger than the old Sun. And older. What's the gas mean?

It's a nebula. Gas left after a star blows up. Goes supernova.

Megan tried to imagine our Sun detonating one lazy afternoon and couldn't. She had slid from a place full of wonders, planets with rings, moons with jeeps, to a universe of unimaginable violence. She did not like it at all.

How far?

Your star? Don't know. Maybe fifty, a hundred light years.

What is that? A light year? Megan knew it was something bad, something she would rather not know. But she had to know anyway.

The distance light travels in a year. It travels 300,000 kilometres in a second.

We'll never get there. We'll never get back.

We're not travelling at the speed of light. We're far better than that. We're still on that roof, remember? We're travelling at the speed of sight.

I don't—oh!

Somewhere between a nameless blue star and a drifting nebula Megan felt a strange and cold pressure on her mind.

Something was in her head.

19

Strangers

Please . . . Megan said.

What's the matter, Meg? Meg . . . ? Kel was weak, frightened and going away.

Something, someone in her head flipping through her mind like a gambler shuffling cards. So fast and so excited, a lizard chasing a new fly.

Aabirdbegcoggirlmalemailwalkflybird?treegrow computemeganmothercitystoplengthmathematical 1234567890=+%multiplystarrocketSTOPbirthdeath peoplemanyplanetEarthtravelthinkSTOP!smalltiny microbeatomgiantPLEASESTOP!elephantwhale whereenough . . .

And it let go, unclenched its fist on Megan's mind, stroked the panic and drifted away. Megan was no longer rushing toward the blue star, just floating. She wanted to go back but she did not know how. She was more frightened than she thought possible, and called out for Kel.

Stop it. Stop the screaming, Kel said quietly.

I'm not. Something has been in my head.

You were screaming. For a long time. Yes, we've found something. Static in the nebula, I don't know. We'll be right.

But haven't you seen? We have stopped—

123

Hello.

It was like a heavy footprint in Megan's mind, cold, powerful and gentle, a giant whispering to a butterfly.

That wasn't you, was it? Megan said to Kel. But she knew.

No. Shut up. Hello.

We are extremely happy to make contact with you. We apologise for causing distress to you earlier. We hope you will excuse us.

That's all right, isn't it, Meg?

Yes. What are we talking to, Megan thought. But she didn't want to ask.

We were too excited in finding intelligent life in the galaxy to realize that our appearance might alarm that life. Thank you for not withdrawing.

You are not from Earth?

Megan wished that Kel hadn't asked. There was always the faint chance that they had bumped into another couple on another roof looking at the same blue star. Until now.

Earth? You think that it is one of nine planets orbiting around a star on an arm of a galaxy. We do not yet know where this is. We are from a triple star system you do not know in the . centre of the galaxy. We were reaching toward the edge of the galaxy when we found you. We have been reaching for a long time . . .

You are aliens. Megan was compressing a little of the fear and feeling a spark of wonder.

Aliens? Creatures? That is strange.

Kel blundered hastily in. *Sorry sir, we didn't mean to offend you, shut up, Meg!*

Offend? What is that? It is strange that we have been exploring the galaxy for 0.3 of its lifetime, but we have

124

never thought of ourselves as aliens. We have found a mudpool that eats at its rock walls and flows uphill on a sulphur planet, and a net that traps light, and we call them aliens. But now we find life that can call us aliens, and it is super.

Super? thought Kel. Boy, did they ever get into the wrong mind!

Dry up, Kel.

Yes, to you we are aliens, but to us hearing you call us aliens is greater than watching the birth of a star system.

Why?

We are not alone any more.

Megan thought about that. On Earth, people were accustomed to the idea of aliens. Aliens were just round the corner, zooming in on flying saucers, getting stuck when the saucer broke down or left without them, hiding in icebergs or old spaceships, invading or plotting. But what happens when you go out of your home planet to find aliens and there just aren't any?

These people—and they are people, now—have been searching for other people, any sort of people, for what?—millions of years—and they haven't been able to find any at all. Stuck in a great galaxy, alone, like one kid playing in an empty schoolground.

Megan could understand the aliens, and the fear dribbled away.

But why can't we see you? Kel said, a little annoyed.

We're like you, Kel. We are in our city and you are in yours and we can only touch you like this.

125

Oh. Kel felt disappointed. *But what do you look like?*

It is very difficult to tell you in your own images.

I don't understand.

You think of heads. We do not know what this is. Foot, leg, hand, food, we do not know what these are. What is breathing, hearing, smelling? We understand 'seeing', but we cannot comprehend the eye. You are near to us, we think, with your images of crystals and electricity, but to you they are completely separate and something you make as you make metal. It is very difficult.

Megan looked around her at the bright burning suns, at the purple curtain of the nebula, at a distant flashing star. She was in a quiet conversation with a creature she could not see, could not even imagine, and she did not know how she felt about it.

But Kel rushed on. *That's great! Crystal people. What colour are you?*

People? Colour? As in light through a prism?

I suppose.

It does not matter. It depends on which of our three suns is nearest. What is wrong?

Megan waited for Kel to answer before she realized the alien was speaking to her.

Oh, sorry. I was laughing, or something. I just stopped being frightened, that's all.

Frightened?

Yes sir, you cannot know what it means. I thought for a while that you were going to eat us or something—

Meg!

Eat?

But that's silly, isn't it? We're so different from you

126

that you just can't want anything from us. Like a tiger and a flower.

The alien gently flipped through Megan's mind in search for tigers, flowers and eating. *Oh*, it said, and it may have been in disappointment, as if it were no nearer to understanding Megan.

Three suns? Kel had been picturing the alien's planet from the moment the suns were mentioned. An old desert landscape with no night, five dark moons sailing across the sky, cities with jewelled minarets . . . *It'd be great to see them.*

You would like to come to our city? The alien seemed a little surprised.

Better than anything! Hey. Meg?

Ah, yes. Yes. But can we?

It may be possible. If we linked with you here we could carry you back home with us. We could show you our city, our civilisation, the planets and stars of the centre of the galaxy, and you could tell us everything about your planet. Your arrival in our city would be the most important moment in its history and we would begin to learn of each other. We would form a friendship and an understanding that would last until the end of the galaxy . . .

That big?

For us, it is that important. You are intelligent life.

Not that intelligent. You would think that we are stupid lumps in your city.

Oh no. You are intelligence from cell life and you can talk with us. You are different, that is all.

Megan thought of a great silver city wall with its gates flung wide. Ambassador from Earth, that's what you'll be. No, First Ambassador from Earth to the Empire of the Crystal People. You'll be in

127

all the history books back home. TV, newspapers, but you'll have to write a book about what you are going to see. Kel can do that. At least he can help.

Megan felt the softest tug at the back of her mind, a tickle like the memory of a long forgotten story.

I'm ready. Take me to your leader! said Kel.

Something warm slipped softly between Megan and the stars. She was beginning to move again, and the tickle had stopped.

Stop! Megan jerked her sight about in panic. *Let me go!*

Come on, Meg, let's go. Kel sounded a little disgusted.

Just stop a minute—please!

The warmth slid away and the movement stopped.

There is something wrong? said the alien.

Kel, how do we get back? I can only just feel the magnet now. If we go on won't we lose it? And without the magnet we'll never get back to us. Will we?

Ah, come on. We can go back any time, can't we?

Oh no, said the alien. *It will be too far. We are now at full stretch. But we can give you everything you want in our city.*

Just hang on a bit. Did you get that, Meg?

Yes.

You don't like it?

Do you?

I'm thinking.

Megan concentrated on the back of her mind until she could feel a whisper of the tug. But maybe she didn't need the tug after all. The tug meant the dirty narrow streets of the suburb, Dad sliding about and maybe trying to get a piece of the family, Mum yelling, the Goblin wrecking the house. She'd still be called The Witch and ol' Rog would always be hanging about. The same thing, year after year.

But up ahead there was an adventure that nobody had ever taken. An alien civilisation thousands of years ahead of Earth, with the ability to sweep most of the galaxy, maybe with you on their back. And the cities they would have built. Go there, and suddenly you're a queen, an empress from a distant and savage planet . . .

I'm going, said Kel.

You're sure?

I haven't got anything going for me back there. My parents, well you know what they're like, they'll be glad that I'm gone. And Alcatraz—no thanks. Nan . . . He stopped for a moment and a star blinked.

I miss her. So much. Before you she was the only person to understand what I am, not a freak, just something different. She was a mate, a teacher, a sister. Just an old woman in a tin shed by the river and now she's gone . . . Doesn't matter. But what do I have to go back to? Coming?

I don't think so. Sorry Kel.

You know what you're missing?

Touch your nose.

Eh?

I was trying to do it a few seconds ago. You know you can't.

We know that. So what?

That's what it'll be like with the aliens. We can go with them, but all we can do is watch.

Sure, but it will be watching things that nobody has

ever seen before, stars exploding, great cities, black holes.
You'd give all that up to play basketball?

Megan thought quietly as she drifted between
the nebula and a dying star.

Balin Dock or the universe? It comes down to
that. The clashing aromas of the cooking of the
Osborne couple, Mrs Fahed and the Chows against
watching a supernova? Watching Laslo build his
wall and paint a new picture on it, against exploring a great alien city? Listening to Goblin wailing
against seeing the centre of the galaxy, where stars
are packed together like lollies in a jar. Come on,
scaredycat, there's no contest.

But there's more, isn't there? Cooking aromas—
you won't smell anything out there, ever. Won't
smell the salt air and the new grass in your little
park, won't hear Judy singing while Laslo builds,
won't taste any more pizza pies, won't feel the
rough bumps of the basketball on your fingertips.

And you'll never know how things will work
out around the place. Will Rosalind and Peter leave
home while the parents fight over a handspan of
land? Will Laslo and Judy become friends? Will
Adrian give up the car? Will Roger become an
actor. Will Alfred ever stop looking for clippers?

Maybe you'd see Goblin write his first word.
Maybe Mum will stop shouting, forget Dad and
start treating you like a friend, not a kid. But you
have to be there.

And maybe Megan Dawson's Allstars will
finally obliterate Captain Alice and Hornsey's Has-
beens. Maybe you'll grow up and become the
mayor and straighten Victor Street and close down
Alcatraz. But you have got to be there.

130

I'm going back, Kel.

Well, I guess that's it. I'm going to miss you . . .

Kel and Megan hung between stars in silence, both looking ahead at the blue star.

You have decided? the alien said.

Yeah, we have decided. Megan goes back home and I come with you.

You can do that? The splitting of the intellect?

We're very clever, we lower life forms. Let's go. See you Meg. Sometime.

Kel!

Megan tried to shout, tried to haul him back for long enough for her to change his mind. But he and the alien were gone, and she was left drifting alone toward the nebula.

20
Alone

There's nobody out there any more, Megan thought. She could see a finger of the nebula brushing a glowering red star, close enough to give the star the beginnings of a shape but not close enough to make it seem solid. There was a cluster of bright white stars clear of the nebula, a sea of stars below her, an inky stain flung at some brilliant sparks, but everything was so far away and so different. The constellations she had seen from her wharfside park had been twisted and stretched until she could not recognise anything.

She was stranded in a strange midnight sky, lost and terribly alone. She could not feel the faintest touch of the magnet this time.

Kel . . . She called his name once, but the thought died in her mind. There was nothing there now. It was like shouting into a bottomless pit, worse. In a pit you could talk to the echo. Here there was nothing at all. She was going to drift between stars forever now, unable to go home, unable even to find it among the stars.

No. Oh please no.

Megan tried to cry, and couldn't. She tried to

close her eyes, and couldn't. She tried to scream and couldn't hear herself.

And then she began to think that she was moving.

She stopped fighting in her mind and wondered. Why did she feel motion? There was no breeze to feel, she had no body to feel it with, there was no movement in the stars . . . But there must be.

She saw two stars very close to each other near the blue star, looked around them and when she returned to the spot there were not two stars, but one with a hump.

The magnet, she thought with a wash of trembling relief. It has come back!

A minute later she felt a tickle in the back of her mind, then a tug and she was a fish, being reeled in across the galaxy. She turned carefully to watch fading stars tumbling from her sight and a small, quiet star begin to grow.

She saw a wall of ice asteroids, black ice spread thinly across the black night, then she was among them and through them. She remembered something about a breeding place for comets but there was no time to wonder about it. The little star was yellowing and growing into a disc. The dim crescent of a distant planet slid beneath her, then Saturn cut its rings across a constellation, this time further away.

The star had become a sun and a planet with its moon rolling, sparkling, in its glare. A small blue planet with a moon of yellowed flour.

We're getting there! Megan thought. Then, with a touch of sorrow: I'm getting there.

The sun was now a controlled explosion in the

centre of the sky, dominating the pinprick stars around it and whitening the plains of the Moon as Megan rushed past. The Earth was a swirl of white cloud over blue, with just a touch of brown. The Earth roared toward Megan, blotting out the stars, the sun, everything.

Too fast, too fast.

The long coastline, the twinkling city, Dalgleish Street with the shiny blue car outside the woolstore and two men breaking in, the roof and lying on the old platform . . .

Megan gasped. She felt the hard ridges on the back of her head, felt herself flowing into her body, the tingling of a foot, the twinge of a thumb.

Then she heard a door splinter below her and staggered to her feet.

'Come on, Kel!' she shouted. 'They're here!'

Megan ran to the hatch and skidded down the rungs as the Hunters pounded up the stairs beneath her. She took a fast little run to the old lift well and clambered down it as the first man reached the top floor.

'He's not here, the hell with it.' The first man flashed his torch about the floor, wavering the beam over the shelves of yellowed paper and sweeping it across the chute, just under Megan's feet.

The second man flicked his torch higher and caught the table. 'He's here all right. He's lived here.' The beam rested on crumpled paper, pie backing and some cheese rinds. 'Maybe the roof.'

The Hunters raced up the rungs and disappeared into the moonlight. Megan started to climb out of the chute, but she hesitated. She was still clinging to the bars on the side of the well when the men thundered clumsily from the roof.

'Almost went through the roof then. It's for monkeys.'

'Bloody kids.'

'What do we do now, then?'

'Thought we had him that time. We just keep on looking.'

'He might've gone bush.'

'Might've. Ah, let's call it a day.'

And the Hunters left the warehouse.

Megan watched them go and climbed back to the roof. There was no sign of Kel, there was nothing on the roof but the old wood pallet and a little ash swirling on the iron.

21
Message

For the first time in several weeks Megan was walking slowly up Dalgleish Street and she did not like the feeling. She had Roger with her and she could feel the sun on her back and smell the blossom in the air but the street still had that bleak, hollow feeling, like a cemetery at night or Dad's empty cupboard.

Oh, things were getting back to normal. The strands of her life that had pulled her back from somewhere out there were wrapping around her, bowling her along. Sometimes, on bright and busy afternoons, she would even forget about Kel and the stars. But not for long and not in Dalgleish Street.

Before Roger had led her into the street she had been thinking about a row she'd won with Mum and she wanted to keep thinking that way. She had complained about spending all her time with Goblin, and to her surprise Mum had conceded a point. Mum was now handling Goblin and would work out things with Mrs Gleason to get Megan more free time. The other day she'd seen, and actually half-waved at Dad in the street. Things were getting better.

'Pretty rotten, wasn't it?' Roger said unhappily.

Megan used the chance to take her eyes from the woolstore. 'What, the play?' He was getting better, too.

'That too. But mainly me.'

'No, you were all right.' Or perhaps she was getting more tolerant with her advancing age.

'Oh, get out of it.'

'No really. You were a little nervous, that's all.'

'Nervous? I was scared stiff.'

Megan stopped across the street from the woolstore. The door and the chute from the footpath were wide open and three men were carrying planks into the building from a parked truck. The woolstore, with its shadowed corners, mysterious rows of curling papers and the rabbit warren of chutes, elevators and cobweb stairs, was changing into several flats. Roger had been right and Megan did not know how to feel about it.

But everything was changing now. Goblin was waddling about the house like a crazy robot; Adrian was rebuilding his car with the wheels removed; Laslo had not painted his new wall because Judy was not giving him enough time on his own; Captain Alice had dropped basketball to help out with a baby sister; Mrs Fahed and the Chows stopped fighting over their front fence but Rosalind and Peter had left. And a new family from Laos had moved into Bates Street. The changing, the little mysteries, never stop.

'What happened to that funny mate of yours?' said Roger.

'My funny mate is you. Who else?' But she knew.

'The kid who fouled up the games arcade.'

'Oh.' Megan gave a long look at the woolstore and walked towards Alfred, as always staring at the harbour. 'I don't know, Roger. He just disappeared.'

She had stared at the sky and waited for Kel to say something for many nights. And received nothing. She thought of finding out where Kel's parents lived, but they didn't like him and he didn't like them. What could she tell them that the Alcatraz people wouldn't. He was missing, no we don't know where he is, and no we don't know whether he is alive or dead. Perhaps she should find out what happened to Nan . . .

'Well at least those odd cops have gone away. Wonder if they ever caught him.'

'No. Ah—I don't think so.'

Megan looked up at the rich blue sky. What happened, Kel? Are you still up there? What do I do, Kel, do I tell them where we've been? Do I tell we've found people up there?

She lowered her gaze to Alfred. She saw him smile and stare at his clipper ships, at a harbour filled with tall ships, a street cluttered with carts laden with wool bales and hauled by bullocks and draft horses—and felt a sudden chill.

Is it like that, Kel? Are you looking at a city half a galaxy away, pretending you are seeing this street but knowing you cannot ever come back?

Roger was speaking to her but the words were suddenly cut off.

Meg . . .

Megan stopped breathing. A very faint voice, so excited it squeaked like a mouse.

Meg, it's not a planet. Nothing like that . . . The voice was fading syllable by syllable, soft as a breeze, the tickling of a hair.

Megan closed her eyes and forced her mind to listen.

. . . a city in the stars . . .

Megan screwed up her eyes. *What do I do, Kel? Do I come up and try to find you? Or do I sit here and wait?*

But that was all.

Megan slowly opened her eyes and Alfred was looking at her. For a long moment the man who saw the past smiled in sympathy at the girl who saw the future.

About the Author

Alan Baillie was born in Scotland in 1943 and lived in Britain until he was seven, when he moved with his family to Australia. On leaving school he worked as a journalist and travelled extensively. He now lives in Sydney with his wife and two children and writes full time.

He is the author of five highly acclaimed novels for children: *Adrift* (shortlisted for the Children's Book of the Year 1985), *Little Brother* (Highly Commended, Children's Book of the Year 1986), *Riverman* (winner of the IBBY Honour Diploma [Australia] 1988 and shortlisted for the Children's Book of the Year 1987), *Eagle Island* and *Megan's Star* (shortlisted for the Children's Book of the Year 1989 and the 1989 NSW Premier's Literary Award).

His first picture book, *Drac and the Gremlin* illustrated by Jane Tanner, was joint winner of the Children's Picture Book of Year Award for 1989.

Also by Allan Baillie

Adrift

'Flynn . . .' Sally's voice was soft and serious. She was looking over her shoulder. 'We're going away.' And so the terrifying adventure began.

Flynn hadn't looked forward to a morning on the beach looking after his little sister. But then they found the old crate, bobbing among the rocks, and for Flynn the crate, became a pirate ship and he was a pirate captain sailing away from all the problems at home and from a Dad who'd become boring and miserable and unfair.

Too late Flynn realised that strong currents had pulled the crate away from the shore and that he, Sally and their cat were adrift, helpless and at the mercy of the sea.

Faced suddenly with the responsibility for keeping himself and Sally alive Flynn finds in himself an unexpected strength and a will to survive and he comes to respect and understand his little sister and his Dad.

This is both a gripping adventure story and a sensitive portrayal of the tensions of family life.

Heard about The Puffin Club?

... it's a way of finding out more about Puffin books and authors, of winning prizes (in competitions), sharing jokes, a secret code, and perhaps seeing your name in print! When you join you get a copy of our magazine, *Puffinalia,* sent to you four times a year, a badge and a membership book. For details of subscription and an application form, send a stamped addressed envelope to:

The Australian Puffin Club
Penguin Books Australia Limited
PO Box 257
Ringwood
Victoria 3134